THE LAST DRINK

FATE IN A GLASS...

KUNWAR ANKUR

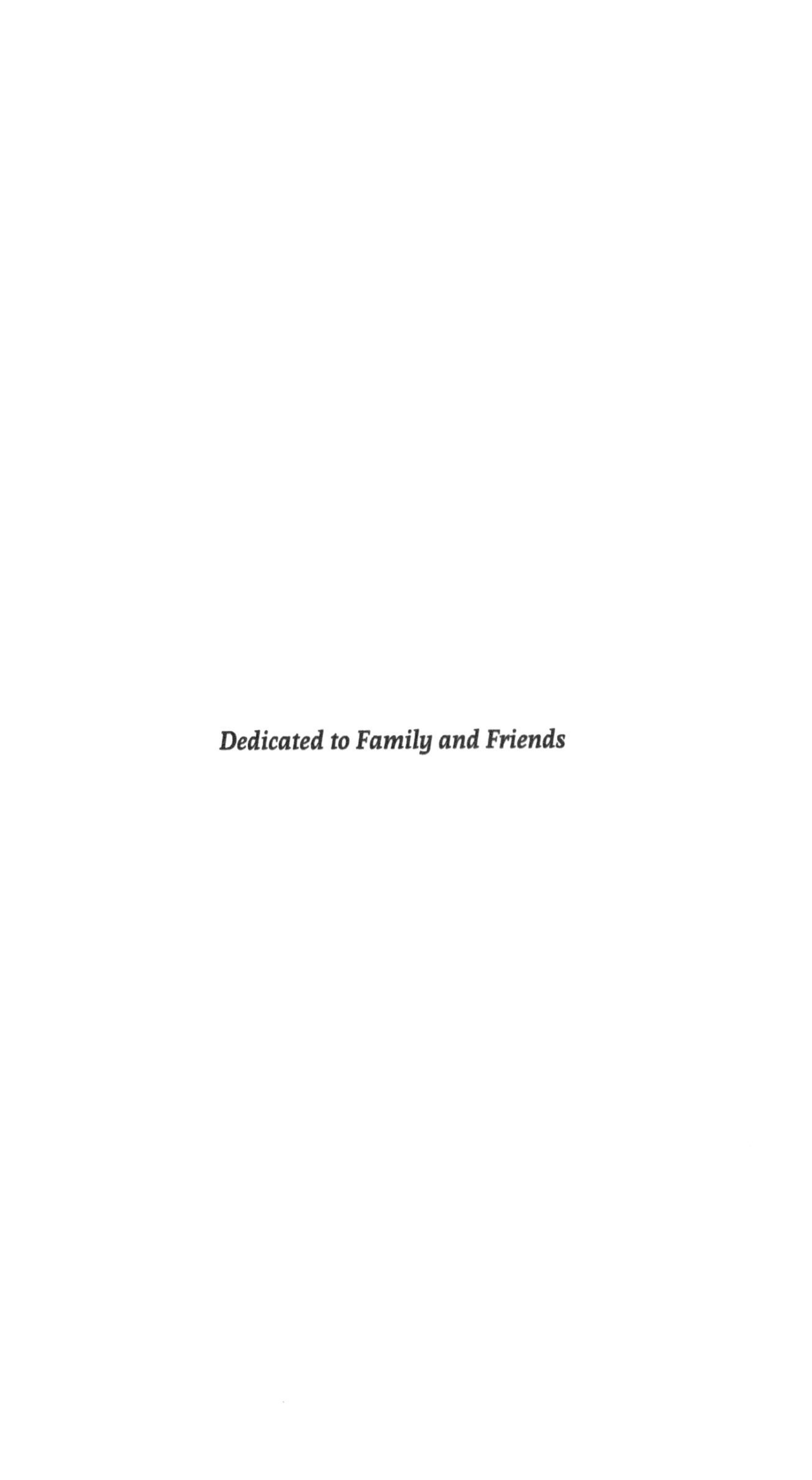

Dedicated to Family and Friends

Contents

Foreword

Dreams don't die all at once. They fade, piece by piece, slipping away until there's nothing left to hold onto.

The Last Drink is a story about dreams, but not the kind that come true effortlessly. It is about the weight of ambition, the cost of chasing something that always feels just out of reach. It is about a boy who once believed he was destined for greatness and a man who, somewhere along the way, lost himself trying to find it.

Ashutosh Rana's journey is not one of meteoric success or grand triumph. Instead, it is a story of struggle—the slow unraveling of a dreamer, the seductive pull of escape, and the brutal reality of addiction. It is about the battle between hope and despair, between the desire to hold on and the temptation to let go.

This book does not offer easy answers. Life rarely does. It does not paint a picture of recovery as a smooth, redemptive arc, nor does it indulge in tragedy for the sake of it. Instead, it lingers in the ambiguity of choice—the space between falling and rising, between succumbing and surviving.

As you turn these pages, you will walk with Ashutosh through the crowded streets of Mumbai, through casting rooms filled with rejection, through dimly lit bars where escape is poured by the glass. You will sit with him in his loneliest moments, feel the sting of lost friendships, the ache of unmet expectations, the weight of the past pressing down on him.

And in the end, when he lifts that final drink, you will wonder—as he does—what comes next.

There are no neat endings here. Only the quiet, haunting moment where everything hangs in the balance. Perhaps that is the truest reflection of life itself.

Preface

I have always been fascinated by stories that don't just entertain but linger—stories that leave questions unanswered, that stay with the reader long after the final page. **The Last Drink** was born from that fascination.

At its heart, this book is about the fragile line between ambition and self-destruction. It follows Ashutosh Rana, a man who once carried dreams too big for the world to ignore, only to find himself swallowed by the very city he believed would make him a star. It is about the intoxicating allure of escape and the quiet, painful struggle of trying to reclaim oneself.

While writing this story, I wanted to explore more than just addiction—I wanted to capture the feeling of being lost. Of standing at the edge of something irreversible. Of wondering if it's already too late to turn back. But above all, I wanted this book to feel real. Not just in its setting or its characters, but in its emotional depth—the suffocating loneliness, the small moments of hope, the weight of choices that define a life.

This is not a story of clear victories or devastating defeats. It is a story of a man suspended between the two, caught in a moment that could change everything—or nothing at all.

I do not know what Ashutosh chooses in the end. Perhaps even he doesn't.

And maybe, that's the point.

Acknowledgements

Writing **The Last Drink** has been a journey—one filled with reflection, struggle, and a deep dive into the fragile complexities of human nature. This book would not have been possible without the support, inspiration, and encouragement of so many people.

First and foremost, I want to thank my readers. Whether you stumbled upon this book by chance or followed its journey from the beginning, your time and engagement mean everything. Stories truly come alive when they find a place in someone's heart, and I am grateful that you chose to walk this path with Ashutosh.

To those who have ever battled their own demons—whether addiction, failure, or the haunting weight of unfulfilled dreams—this book is for you. Your resilience, your struggles, and your courage to keep moving forward, even when the road is uncertain, have shaped this story more than you know.

To my friends and family, thank you for your unwavering belief in me. For the conversations that sparked new ideas, for the moments of encouragement when doubt crept in, and for reminding me why stories matter. Your support has been my foundation.

A heartfelt thank you to my mentors, teachers, and everyone who has ever influenced my writing in any way. Every lesson, every word of wisdom, and every push toward storytelling has played a part in shaping this book.

To every dreamer who has dared to chase something bigger than themselves, to those who have faced rejection but continued anyway, and to anyone who has ever found themselves lost between who they were and who they hoped to become—this book is, in many ways, yours too.

And finally, to the city of Mumbai—its chaos, its beauty, its unforgiving nature, and its quiet moments of magic. This story could not have existed anywhere else.

Thank you all.

Happy Reading.

~ Kunwar Ankur

Prologue

Mumbai—the city of dreams, where ambition collides with reality, where the streets whisper promises of stardom but swallow countless nameless faces in the process.

Ashutosh Rana had once believed he would be different. He had arrived with nothing but a suitcase full of hope and a heart unwilling to accept defeat. The city had welcomed him with its deceptive charm, pulling him into a whirlwind of auditions, rejections, fleeting moments of validation, and the slow, merciless erosion of everything he had once believed in.

Somewhere along the way, the fire inside him dimmed. The bright-eyed boy who had memorized monologues in front of a cracked mirror faded into someone unrecognizable—a man drowning in his own vices, reaching for a bottle instead of a script.

What had started as an escape had become a prison.

Now, he sat alone in a dimly lit room, staring at the last drink of his life.

The weight of his past bore down on him—the laughter of old friends who had long since given up on him, the disappointed silence of his parents, the echoes of every 'maybe next time' he had ever heard from a casting director.

This drink could be the end.

Or the beginning.

Outside, the city pulsed with indifference, uncaring of whether he rose or fell.

Inside, a choice remained.

And as his fingers tightened around the glass, the story began.

1

The Burden of Expectations

Expectations are like invisible chains—sometimes woven with love, sometimes with duty, but always binding. They shape us before we even understand who we are, dictating the paths we walk and the choices we make. Some carry these expectations like armor, embracing them as their purpose, while others feel them as shackles, restraining their true desires.

In a world where success is often measured by stability rather than passion, dreams can become mere whispers, drowned out by the voices of tradition and responsibility. Families, society, and even our own fears push us toward paths deemed 'safe,' leaving little room for the unpredictable journey of ambition. The weight of these expectations can be crushing, forcing individuals to choose between fulfilling the hopes of others or pursuing the uncertain call of their own dreams.

But what happens when the burden becomes too heavy? When the heart refuses to follow the well-paved road laid out for it? When the fire of ambition refuses to be extinguished, despite the odds? Some surrender, letting the current of obligation sweep them away. Others fight—struggling, stumbling, and sometimes even falling. Yet, in that battle between expectation and passion, a person's true story is written.

ꝁꝁꝁ

Ashutosh Rana grew up in the bustling yet tradition-bound lanes of Gorakhpur, where life hummed with the sounds of vendors calling out their wares, children chasing each other through dusty streets, and elders gathering in tea stalls to discuss everything from politics to family legacies. It was a place where time moved forward, yet traditions held firm, wrapping around families like invisible chains. Here, dreams were not seen as individual pursuits; they were family investments, carefully cultivated to yield the ultimate reward—stability, respect, and approval from society.

Every household had its own version of success, but the underlying theme remained the same: education led to security, and security led to honor. For most parents, the pinnacle of achievement was securing a government job or excelling in a profession like engineering or medicine. To dare to dream beyond this structure was considered reckless, even selfish.

As the only son in his family, Ashutosh bore the full weight of these expectations. His father, Rajendra Rana, was a man of discipline, his words carrying the sharpness of unquestionable authority. A self-made man, he had worked tirelessly to build a respectable life for his family, and he expected Ashutosh to do the same—only through the 'right' path. To him, his son was more than just an individual with aspirations; he was the torchbearer of the family name, the one who would elevate their status with his success.

"An IIT degree is not just a piece of paper, Ashu," his father often said, his voice firm, unwavering. *"It's a guarantee—a guarantee that you will never have to struggle, that you will always be respected. What more could a man ask for?"*

Engineering was not a mere profession in his father's eyes; it was a legacy, a mark of intelligence, a ticket to prosperity. The thought of Ashutosh choosing anything else was inconceivable.

His mother, Sunita Rana, was gentler in her approach but no less firm in her beliefs. She did not issue ultimatums like her husband, but her quiet insistence carried just as much weight. To her, an engineering degree wasn't just about prestige—it was about protection. She had seen enough hardship in life to know that dreams, especially uncertain ones, could crumble in an instant. She feared instability, the unpredictability of professions like acting, where success was a gamble few could win.

"Beta," she would say softly as she ran her fingers through his hair, *"this world is not kind to those who walk an uncertain path. A steady job means a steady life. Acting... it's not for people like us. Why struggle when you can have security?"*

Her words were never harsh, never dismissive, but they held an unshakable truth—one rooted in fear, in the stories of those who had dared to chase dreams and returned empty-handed.

And so, from the moment Ashutosh was old enough to understand words like *career* and *future*, his path had been set before him, carved out with precision. His childhood was filled with textbooks, mock tests, and coaching classes that stretched late into the evening. While other children played cricket in the narrow bylanes, he sat in his room solving math problems. While his friends talked about movies and weekend plans, his conversations at home revolved around entrance exams, cut-off marks, and the fierce competition that awaited him.

"Do you know how many students appear for IIT every year?" his father would remind him, his voice carrying the weight of expectation. *"Lakhs, Ashu. And only the best make it. You have to be the best."*

There was no room for doubt, no space for alternatives. His life was a carefully constructed script, one that left no space for improvisation. His future had been decided for him—long before he had a chance to dream of one for himself.

ᗷᗷᗷ

But Ashutosh was different. While his father saw equations and formulas as the key to success, Ashutosh saw the world in scenes and dialogues, in fleeting moments captured through words, expressions, and emotions. Numbers never fascinated him the way stories did. His friends would lose themselves in the logic of physics and the complexities of calculus, but Ashutosh found himself drawn to something else—the magic of storytelling, the way a simple monologue could make people laugh, cry, or feel something so deeply that it lingered long after the credits rolled.

For his father, success was something measurable—a rank in an entrance exam, a stable job, a respectable salary. It was tangible, something that could be presented with degrees and certificates, something society could validate. *"Life is about security, Ashu,"* his father would often say, adjusting his glasses as he read the newspaper. *"When you have a job, a good salary, a reputation—only then do people respect you. That's what matters."*

But Ashutosh's idea of achievement was different. To him, success was not about security—it was about significance. It wasn't about numbers on a report card; it was in the way an audience held its breath during an intense scene, in the thunderous applause that erupted when a performance resonated with people's hearts. It was in the power of cinema—the ability to make people feel, to transport them to different worlds, to leave an imprint long after the screen faded to black.

His heart belonged to the grandeur of Bollywood, where emotions were larger than life, where dreams were woven into stories that touched millions. He admired the legends who had once been nobodies—those who had arrived in Mumbai with nothing but determination and had fought against all odds to carve a name for themselves. He saw himself in their struggles, in their rejections, in their resilience.

"Amitabh Bachchan was rejected so many times before he got his break," Ashutosh once argued at the dinner table. *"Shah Rukh Khan came to Mumbai with no connections, no godfather. Look at them now!"*

His father scoffed, shaking his head. *"For every Amitabh and Shah Rukh, there are thousands who come back home empty-handed, Ashu. Have you ever thought about that? What will you do if you fail? You think you can pay bills with dreams?"*

His mother sighed, placing an extra roti on his plate. *"Beta, it's not that we don't want you to be happy,"* she said gently. *"But acting... it's not for people like us. It's for the rich, for those who can afford to take risks. You need to think about your future practically."*

Practically. That word haunted him. It was the shield his family used to dismiss his passion, the wall that stood between him and his dreams.

While others read textbooks, he memorized dialogues. While his classmates prepared for IIT entrance exams, he stood in front of the mirror, perfecting his expressions, mimicking the stars he idolized. He studied actors the way his father wanted him to study engineering—watching how they moved, how they delivered a line, how they made an audience believe in their characters.

"Papa, I don't want to be an engineer," he had blurted out one evening, his voice firm despite the nervous pounding in his chest.

His father didn't look up from his newspaper. *"Then what do you want to do?"*

"I want to be an actor."

Silence. His mother looked at him as if he had spoken in a foreign language. His sisters exchanged nervous glances, their eyes pleading with him not to push too far. His father, after a long pause, let out a slow, heavy breath and finally met his son's gaze.

"An actor?" he repeated, as if the very word was an insult. He placed the newspaper down carefully, folding it neatly. *"And how exactly do you plan to survive in Mumbai? Do you have any idea how many people go there every day with the same dream? Ninety-nine percent of them return home with nothing but regret."*

"And what if I succeed?" Ashutosh challenged, his hands clenched under the table.

His father's voice remained calm, but his words were like iron. *"Success in this world is not about dreams, Ashu. It's about certainty. And there is no certainty in what you are chasing."*

That night, as he lay in bed staring at the ceiling, he realized something—his dream was fragile in a world that valued practicality. And in his home, where ambition was measured in career stability, his love for acting was not seen as a goal but as a distraction, a foolish indulgence that had no place in the real world.

But no matter how much they tried to silence it, the fire within him refused to go out.

ϷϷϷ

His two elder sisters were his silent allies, the only ones in the family who truly saw him for who he was. Unlike their parents, who dismissed his love for cinema as a childish distraction, they understood that acting wasn't just a passing fancy for Ashutosh—it was his calling, the fire that lit up his soul.

They had witnessed his passion in ways no one else had. They had seen him lock himself in his room for hours, standing in front of the mirror, practicing monologues with the intensity of a seasoned actor. They had heard his voice shift seamlessly between emotions—anger, sorrow, triumph—as if he were already performing in front of a camera. They had watched him analyze movies with a deep admiration, breaking down an actor's expressions, the subtlety in their gestures, the weight of a pause between words.

"Did you see how Irrfan Khan delivered that line?" he would say excitedly after watching a film. *"He didn't even raise his voice, but you could feel the tension. That's real acting, didi!"*

His sisters, Rachna and Neha, would exchange amused glances, smiling at his enthusiasm. *"You don't just watch movies, Ashu. You dissect them,"* Rachna would tease.

"That's because he's not just watching," Neha would add softly. *"He's living it."*

They knew, better than anyone, that Ashutosh was different. While they had learned to silence their own dreams, to accept the roles assigned to them by their family, they couldn't ignore the fire burning inside their younger brother. They saw how restless he became whenever discussions about engineering took over the dinner table, how he would bite his tongue to keep from arguing, how he would clench his fists whenever their father spoke about IIT as if it were the only path to success.

"Ashu, why don't you just tell Papa how you feel?" Rachna asked him one night, as they sat on the terrace under the dim glow of the streetlights.

He let out a bitter chuckle. *"And say what? That I want to be an actor? That I want to go to Mumbai and struggle for years, waiting for one audition that might never come? Papa will laugh in my face. Or worse... he'll be disappointed."*

Neha sighed. *"You know he just wants what's best for you, right?"*

"No, he wants what's best for him," Ashutosh corrected. *"He wants to be able to tell people, 'My son is an IITian.' He wants certainty. But I don't want to live a life where every day feels the same, where I wake up and do something I don't love just because it's safe."*

His sisters understood. They understood because they had been raised in the same house, under the same expectations. They had dreams once, too, dreams they had quietly set aside in the name of family duty.

Rachna, who had always loved writing, had once dreamed of becoming a journalist, traveling to different cities, telling stories that mattered. But she had accepted an arranged marriage before she even had the chance to explore that path. Neha, with her love for painting, had once imagined showcasing her art in galleries, but practicality had forced her into a teaching job instead. They had made their choices, choices that felt less like decisions and more like inevitabilities.

And now, they saw Ashutosh standing at the same crossroads, only he was not ready to surrender just yet.

So, they supported him in whatever small ways they could. A knowing glance when their father dismissed his acting ambitions. A reassuring squeeze of his hand when he looked defeated. A whispered word of encouragement when he doubted himself.

"If anyone can do this, it's you, Ashu," Rachna told him one evening as they stood by the kitchen, away from their parents' ears.

Neha placed a comforting hand on his shoulder. *"Just promise us one thing,"* she said. *"If you ever get the chance to chase this dream... don't hesitate. Don't let anyone stop you."*

They couldn't openly challenge the expectations set by their parents, but they could be his quiet strength. They could be the only ones who truly believed in his dream, even when the rest of the world refused to.

ppp

The weight of expectation wrapped around Ashutosh like an ever-tightening noose, pulling him deeper into a life he did not want. His home, though warm and familiar, often felt like a battlefield—his dreams and his family's expectations clashing in a war with no truce.

Every dinner conversation became a strategy session, dissecting his future as if it were a chessboard where only one move led to victory—engineering. His father sat at the head of the table, his voice steady and authoritative.

"I spoke to Sharma ji today," he announced, tearing off a piece of roti. *"His son has joined a coaching institute in*

Kota. He says the best teachers are there. If you start preparing seriously now, you can get into IIT Delhi."

Ashutosh forced himself to nod, his stomach churning. He had lost count of how many times these conversations had taken place, how many times his future had been decided for him without his consent.

"Papa, I—" he started hesitantly, but before he could finish, his mother cut in.

"Ashu beta, you know your father only wants what's best for you," she said gently, placing a hand on his. *"An IIT degree will open doors. A good job, a good salary, a secure life... Isn't that what every boy dreams of?"*

"No, Ma," he wanted to say. *"That's not what I dream of."*

But he remained silent, swallowing his words along with the bite of food that suddenly felt tasteless.

Whenever he dared to mention acting, it was dismissed with amused chuckles or stern disapproval.

"Ashutosh, stop watching those films and focus on your studies," his father would say, shaking his head. *"Actors are born into the industry or get lucky. What makes you think you'll succeed?"*

"Because I want it more than anything," Ashutosh would mutter under his breath, but his father was never interested in hearing his answers.

And when he did try to argue, when he dared to mention the stars who had come from nothing—Nawazuddin Siddiqui, Rajkummar Rao, Ayushmann Khurrana—his father had a counter ready.

"For every one actor who makes it, there are ten thousand who don't," he said one evening, his voice edged with finality. *"Do you know how many young men go to Mumbai every year? And do you know how many come back with nothing but shattered dreams? You think you're special? You think hard*

work is enough?"

Ashutosh clenched his fists under the table.

"But, Papa—"

"Enough!" His father's voice cut through the air, sharp and unwavering. *"Dreams don't feed families. Do you understand that? Acting is not a career. It's a gamble. And we are not gamblers."*

The words stung. They always did.

His mother, though less forceful, echoed the same concerns in a softer way. *"Beta, we've given you the best education we could afford. We just want to see you settled. A stable job, a good home, a family of your own... isn't that what matters?"*

Ashutosh wanted to scream that none of it mattered if he wasn't happy. But instead, he nodded weakly, pushing his food around his plate.

The pressure mounted with every passing day. His parents reminded him constantly of the sacrifices they had made, the dreams they had tied to his success.

"Your father worked day and night to ensure you got into the best schools," his mother would say. *"How will he feel if you throw it all away?"*

"If you waste this opportunity, Ashu, it will break your father's heart," his sister Neha whispered one night.

Guilt weighed on him like an anchor. He loved his parents. He truly did. He wanted to make them proud. But was he willing to lose himself in the process?

The battle inside him raged on. Could he bear the burden of being the son who defied his family's wishes? Or was he destined to follow the path laid out for him, even if it led to a life of quiet suffocation?

And yet, beneath the crushing expectations, beneath the fear and doubt, a quiet rebellion flickered within him—a stubborn belief that his future was meant for something more than equations and calculations. A belief that no matter how much they tried to steer him away, the stage was where he truly belonged.

ᗡᗡᗡ

No matter how many times his father dismissed it as a childish fantasy, no matter how often his mother gently nudged him toward a safer path, Ashutosh knew—his dream was not a fleeting indulgence. It was a fire, consuming him from the inside, a force too powerful to be ignored. It wasn't something he had chosen on a whim; it had chosen him, etched into his soul long before he had even realized it.

Every time he watched a film, he didn't just see actors performing—he felt every flicker of emotion, every shift in expression, every moment of silence that spoke louder than words. A well-delivered dialogue could make his heart race, a single tear on screen could choke him up. He would rewind scenes over and over, not just to watch, but to understand. *"How did the actor's face change when he delivered that line? Why did he pause before speaking? What was it about that moment that made the audience feel something so deeply?*

One evening, as his family sat watching a movie, Ashutosh found himself mesmerized by a powerful monologue. The actor on screen poured his heart into every word, his voice rising and falling like a storm, eyes brimming with raw intensity. Ashutosh's fingers gripped the edge of his chair. *"This... this is what I want to do."*

Lost in the scene, he unconsciously whispered the lines under his breath, his lips moving in sync with the actor's. His sister Neha, sitting beside him, nudged him with a small smile. *"You've already memorized it, haven't you?"*

Ashutosh grinned sheepishly. *"It's not just about memorizing. It's about feeling it."*

But the moment was short-lived. His father, hearing their exchange, scoffed. *"Feeling it?"* he muttered, shaking his head. *"You waste so much time on these films. If only you put half this effort into your studies, you'd already be topping your class."*

His mother sighed, placing a hand on his father's arm. *"Let him enjoy his movies, at least for now,"* she said, though there was an underlying concern in her voice.

Ashutosh clenched his fists. He wanted to argue, to make them understand that this wasn't some silly pastime—this was his life. He wasn't watching movies to escape reality; he was watching them to study, to learn, to prepare.

Late at night, when the house was silent, he would stand in front of his mirror, reenacting scenes with a passion that made his heart race. He would perfect every expression, every pause, every movement until it felt natural.

"Again," he would tell himself. *"Do it again, but this time, mean it."*

And when he got it just right—when the emotion felt real, when he believed in the words he was speaking—he would smile, knowing deep down that this was what he was meant to do.

But dreams like his came at a cost.

He knew that chasing this path meant defying everything his family had planned for him. It meant risking their disappointment, perhaps even their anger. It meant stepping into a world where success was uncertain, where rejection was more common than applause. It meant walking away from the security of a stable career and into the unknown.

"You need to be practical, Ashu," his mother told him one evening as she folded his clothes. *"We don't come from a background where we can afford to chase dreams that have no guarantees."*

"But Ma," he said, his voice quieter than he intended, *"what if this isn't just a dream? What if this is the only thing that makes me feel alive?"*

She paused, looking at him with a softness that made his chest ache. For a brief moment, he thought she understood. But then, with a sigh, she shook her head.

"Life isn't just about feeling alive, beta," she murmured. *"It's about survival."*

Ashutosh turned away, staring at the cracked ceiling of his room that night, his mind racing. Maybe she was right. Maybe life was about survival.

But what was the point of surviving if he couldn't truly live?

And so, despite the fear, despite the weight of his family's expectations pressing down on him, one truth remained unshaken—he would rather struggle for his dreams than live a life that was never meant for him.

2
The Secret Dream

Dreams are fragile things. They begin as whispers, hidden in the quiet corners of the mind, nurtured in stolen moments and secret thoughts. They have no weight, no form—just a feeling, an unshakable pull toward something greater, something beyond the ordinary. In the beginning, they are harmless, no more than fleeting ideas, indulged in between the demands of reality. But the more they are fed, the more they grow, gaining shape, substance, and urgency.

But dreams are also dangerous. They exist in conflict with reality, often at odds with the life already set in motion. They demand courage, defiance, and an unwillingness to conform. And in a world where expectations are law, where the future is a carefully planned blueprint, a dream that dares to deviate is not just risky—it is forbidden.

For some, giving up on a dream is easy. The weight of responsibility is too heavy, the voice of tradition too loud, and the fear of failure too strong. But for others, the dream is relentless. It refuses to be silenced. It survives in the spaces between responsibility and desire, in the silence of the night, in the reflection of a mirror that shows not who a person is—but who they long to become.

And when a dream refuses to die, it turns into something else entirely. A secret. A rebellion. A fire that no amount of expectation can extinguish.

ÞÞÞ

Ashutosh had always been the pride of his family—the boy who aced every exam, the one teachers praised, the son who was destined for something secure, stable, and respectable. From a young age, he had been conditioned to believe that success was a well-defined path: excel in school, secure a seat in IIT, and become an engineer. It was an unspoken rule in the narrow lanes of Gorakhpur, where aspirations rarely extended beyond the confines of a stable profession.

His father often spoke about the power of an IIT degree.

"Do you know how many students in India dream of this, Ashutosh?" his father would say, adjusting his glasses as he scanned the newspaper. *"Once you have that IIT tag, companies will come looking for you. You won't have to run after success—success will run after you."*

Ashutosh would nod, his fingers tightening around the edges of his book. He had heard these words too many times before.

"An IIT engineer," his uncle had once declared during a family gathering, clapping a firm hand on his shoulder. *"The first one in our family. You will make us all proud."*

His mother, though softer in her approach, held the same expectations. When she sat beside him at night, running a gentle hand over his hair, her voice was kind but firm.

"Just a few more years of hard work, beta," she would murmur. *"Once you are settled, everything will be easy. No worries, no struggles. A good job, a happy life."*

Everyone spoke of his future as if it had already been written, as if he had no say in it. IIT was not just a goal; it was a destiny that had been decided for him long before he even understood what it meant.

And so, he played his part.

At school, he was the model student—diligent, disciplined, and always prepared. His teachers admired his focus, his classmates envied his intelligence. When exams came, he secured the highest marks, and when competitions were held, he brought home the trophies.

"You make it look easy, Ashu," his best friend, Raghav, once joked as they walked home from school. *"You were born to crack IIT!"*

Ashutosh forced a smile, but inside, something twisted.

Born to crack IIT.

The words echoed in his mind long after they were spoken, lingering like a truth he didn't want to accept.

ƿƿƿ

Relatives, neighbors, and even shopkeepers who barely knew him would pat his back and remind him that he was different.

"The boy is brilliant," the local grocer often told his customers, his voice brimming with pride as if Ashutosh belonged to him. *"Mark my words, one day, he'll be earning in lakhs!"*

The barber, who had seen him grow from a timid child into a studious teenager, often chimed in when Ashutosh passed by his shop.

"Remember us when you become a big engineer, beta," he would say with a chuckle, the scent of shaving cream thick in the air. *"We'll tell people, 'he used to come here for a two-rupee haircut!'"*

Everyone had a version of his future already mapped out. Their words were filled with expectations, not encouragement. No one asked him what he wanted. They simply assumed.

"Ashutosh, IIT prep must be tough, no?" an elderly neighbor asked one evening as he walked home from school.

"It is," he replied, keeping his voice polite, his expression unreadable.

"Good, good," the old man nodded approvingly. *"Hard work now, easy life later. You're a smart boy, you won't let us down."*

He had been molded into an obedient child, one who never questioned what was expected of him. His father's voice always rang in his ears—*"Keep your head down, study hard, no distractions."*

And so he did.

He excelled in every subject, not because he loved them, but because failure was never an option. His notebooks were always neat, his handwriting impeccable, his answers precise. He memorized formulas and historical dates as if they were scriptures, not daring to falter.

Late at night, when he sat at his desk solving yet another set of physics problems, his mother would peek into the room.

"Go to sleep, beta. Don't strain yourself too much," she would say.

"I'll just finish one more chapter," he always replied, knowing she would smile and walk away, proud of his dedication.

Yet, deep within him, something stirred—something unspoken, something beyond numbers and textbooks.

Because expectations were one thing.

Dreams were another.

And Ashutosh's dreams did not fit within the narrow alleys of Gorakhpur's traditions.

৷৷৷

At night, when the house fell silent and the weight of the day's responsibilities faded, Ashutosh would retreat into his small room, the only space where he could truly be himself. The room was modest—just a wooden cot, a small study table cluttered with books, and a cracked mirror that leaned precariously against the wall. That mirror, flawed and imperfect, was his only confidant. It did not judge him. It did not remind him of his duties. It simply reflected back the version of himself he longed to be.

This was where his secret life began.

He would shut the door carefully, listening for any sound from outside. His parents were in their room, his younger siblings fast asleep. The house was wrapped in a blanket of silence, the only noise coming from the occasional rustling of leaves outside his window. It was the perfect moment—the only moment—when he could let go of the life that was expected of him and step into the one he craved.

Standing before the mirror, he straightened his posture, squared his shoulders, and allowed his face to transform. His eyes, usually weighed down by the exhaustion of studies and responsibilities, would light up with an intensity that no one had ever seen. He wasn't Ashutosh anymore. He was a hero, a lover, a warrior, a villain. He became whoever he wanted to be.

He had memorized countless dialogues from old films, his mind a vault of iconic monologues and dramatic exchanges. He mouthed the words, feeling them rather than just speaking them.

"You think you can break me?" he whispered to his reflection, his voice trembling with emotion. *"No... I have lived through storms, through fire, through betrayal. And yet, here I stand!"*

His voice was low but firm, his expression shifting as he imagined himself on a grand stage, performing under the glow of spotlights. His hands moved expressively, slicing through the dim light of the room, his fingers curling and opening with deliberate precision. His face shifted between emotions he had observed so many times on the silver screen—anger, sorrow, love, triumph. He practiced every gesture, every glance, every breath as if his reflection were a silent audience, watching his transformation from a quiet, studious boy to a man of a thousand roles.

He took a step back, running a hand through his hair, preparing for another scene. His mind raced through the movies he had watched in secret, pulling out the perfect moment, the perfect line.

"You betrayed me," he murmured, his voice dropping into something cold and distant. Then, he let out a bitter laugh, his expression changing instantly. *"But I should have seen it coming. A man who trusts too much... is a fool."*

The words hung in the air, thick with an emotion that didn't belong in this tiny room. If anyone saw him now, they would think he was mad. But this was the only time he felt truly alive.

Sometimes, he would enact entire scenes, moving around the room as if it were a grand stage, his bed serving as a makeshift throne, his books doubling as props. He would pause between performances, analyzing himself in the mirror, perfecting the arch of an eyebrow, the furrow of his brow, the quiver of his lips before a moment of heartbreak. He wasn't just mimicking—he was feeling, living, breathing the emotions that had long been trapped within him.

The world outside his room would never understand. By day, he was the obedient son, the brilliant student, the boy everyone admired. But at night, he was something else—something more.

In front of the cracked mirror, he wasn't bound by expectations. He wasn't limited by the future that had already been decided for him.

In those fleeting moments, he was free.

ᐁᐁᐁ

Books and notebooks lay scattered around his bed, a chaotic mix of academic excellence and artistic rebellion. Neatly written mathematical formulas and physics equations filled the pages meant for his studies, but in between them—scribbled in the margins, hidden in the last pages—were lines of dialogue from movies he had watched in secret. Some were famous monologues, others were his own creations, emotions poured into words that only he would ever read. These stolen moments of creativity were his way of keeping his dream alive, even as reality tried to smother it.

"Ashu, are you writing again?" Rohit whispered, leaning over his shoulder in the classroom. His voice was low, but there was amusement in his tone.

Ashutosh instinctively slammed his notebook shut, his heart pounding. *"Nothing... just some calculations."*

Rohit smirked. *"Oh yeah? Since when do physics equations sound like tragic love stories?"*

"Shut up. If the teacher sees, I'm finished," Ashutosh muttered, stuffing the notebook into his bag.

Rohit chuckled but didn't press further. He knew Ashutosh better than anyone. While others saw him as the ideal student, Rohit saw the restlessness in his eyes, the way he scribbled dialogues when he thought no one was looking, the way his fingers drummed against the desk as if rehearsing an invisible script.

Whenever he could, Ashutosh borrowed DVDs from Rohit, the only person who shared his passion for cinema but lacked the courage to dream beyond the ordinary. The two of them would huddle together at night, watching films in hushed silence, their eyes absorbing every movement, every flicker of emotion on the actors' faces. They weren't just watching; they were studying—dissecting performances, analyzing expressions, memorizing lines that had once echoed in grand cinema halls across the country. Every masterpiece left an imprint on Ashutosh's soul, igniting a fire that burned brighter with each scene.

"See that? The way his eyes move—this is real emotion," Ashutosh whispered, rewinding a scene from an old classic.

Rohit yawned, stretching. *"Dude, you're turning into a full-fledged director now."*

"I'm just trying to understand how actors make you feel something," Ashutosh murmured, his gaze still fixed on the screen.

Rohit shook his head with a lazy grin. *"And I'm just trying to understand how we'll pass tomorrow's math test."*

But the moment the screen went black and the movie ended, reality would come rushing back. The dream had to be folded away like a secret letter, tucked into the hidden corners of his mind.

"Go to sleep now," Rohit mumbled, already lying back on the bed. *"Tomorrow morning, back to IIT prep."*

The words felt like a slap of cold water, dragging Ashutosh back to the life he was supposed to live. He stared at the blank screen for a moment longer, as if willing it to turn back on, to let him stay in that world just a little longer. But dreams could only last so long.

The next morning, he would return to his other role—the one he had been assigned rather than the one he had chosen.

At school, he played his part flawlessly. The diligent student who never missed an assignment, the boy teachers held up as an example.

"Ashutosh, if students like you maintain discipline, IIT is not far," his physics teacher said in class one day, nodding approvingly as he checked his work.

He nodded, forcing a smile, but his mind was elsewhere—somewhere beyond textbooks and exams, somewhere far away from the life everyone expected him to live.

ᐯᐯᐯ

At home, he was the responsible son, the one expected to set the standard for his younger cousins. His father would glance at his books, his eyes filled with the quiet confidence of a man who had mapped out his son's future.

"Just one more year," he said one evening, adjusting his spectacles as he flipped through the pages of a newspaper. *"Once you crack IIT, everything will be set."*

"Yes, Papa," Ashutosh replied automatically, his voice steady. His hands clutched the same books that held his hidden scribbles—formulas on one page, lines from a monologue on the other. One life neatly arranged, the other squeezed into the margins.

His visiting cousin, Anuj, sat nearby, swinging his legs over the edge of the cot. *"Bhaiya, when you become an engineer, will you buy me a bicycle?"*

Ashutosh smiled faintly. *"Of course,"* he said, ruffling Anuj's hair. But his mind wandered—if things were different, if he were free to choose, what would he promise instead?

In every interaction, he carried the weight of his family's expectations, moving through life as if following a script someone else had written for him. His lines were rehearsed, his expressions practiced, his obedience flawless. But deep inside, something rebelled.

His heart didn't belong to textbooks or lectures, nor to the steady, predictable path laid out for him. It belonged to a world where words weren't just spoken but performed, where emotions weren't just felt but lived. A world where he could be anyone—a fearless warrior, a tormented lover, a dreamer chasing the impossible. A world where he could step into a role and become larger than life.

But this wasn't a place for dreams like his. Gorakhpur, with its narrow lanes and narrower expectations, thrived on stability. A dream as uncertain as acting was almost laughable here.

Almost.

Because Ashutosh knew—no matter how much he tried to bury it, no matter how perfectly he played his assigned role—this dream was not something he could abandon. It was not a phase. It was not a childish fantasy.

It was a part of him.

The only thing that truly felt real.

And even if no one else saw it, even if the whole world expected him to be someone else, the reflection in his cracked mirror told him the truth.

Someday, he would have to choose.

3
The Great Rebellion

Some choices are made for you long before you even realize they exist. They are woven into the fabric of your life, hidden within words of praise and gentle reminders, disguised as love and concern. These choices are never truly yours, yet they shape you, mold you, define the person you are expected to become. They come wrapped in expectations—passed down like heirlooms from one generation to the next, each layer of duty and sacrifice adding to their weight.

You grow up believing in them, carrying them like an inheritance you never questioned. You follow the path laid out for you, thinking it is the only road that leads to success, to happiness, to respect. And for a while, you convince yourself that this is enough. That the dreams you were born with can be locked away in the corners of your heart, quiet and forgotten.

But dreams are not meant to be buried. They are restless, persistent. They whisper to you in the dead of night, in moments of solitude, in stolen glances at a world that is not yours but could be.

And then, one day, something shifts. The burden of those inherited choices becomes too heavy to bear. The fear of disappointing those who love you still lingers, but it no longer outweighs the ache of living a life that is not your own.

For Ashutosh, that moment had arrived.

ϸϸϸ

Some storms don't arrive with loud thunder or sudden downpours. Some creep in silently, darkening the sky little by little until you realize the sun is gone.

The tension in the house had been building for weeks, settling into the air like dust in a forgotten room. No one spoke of it, but it was there—hanging over every conversation, lurking in the pauses, waiting for the moment it would finally spill over.

It started with hesitation.

Ashutosh had always known the right things to say, the expected responses that kept the world around him content. But lately, his words stumbled. His voice wavered ever so slightly when his father spoke of IIT, his nods of agreement felt slower, his smiles tighter.

The change was subtle at first. A flicker in his eyes when relatives praised his "bright future." A moment of silence before answering when someone asked about his entrance exam preparations. He still played the part, but the performance was cracking.

His mother noticed first.

Mothers always do.

She saw it in the way he stared at his books—not with the sharp focus that once defined him, but with something else. Something hesitant. Something far away. His eyes no longer scanned the pages with purpose; they wandered, lost in thoughts she could not hear.

"Ashu, are you feeling alright?" she asked one evening as she placed a cup of tea beside him.

"Yeah, Maa. Just tired," he said, forcing a smile. But the way his fingers tapped against his notebook told a different story.

Then came the late nights.

The soft glow of his computer screen became a constant presence, illuminating his face long after the rest of the house had fallen into sleep. His father assumed he was working harder than ever, pushing himself to secure his future.

But Ashutosh wasn't solving equations.

His screen held a different reality—film schools in Mumbai, acting academies, interviews with struggling actors who had defied expectations, who had walked away from certainty to chase something no one believed in. He read their stories with a quiet desperation, hanging onto every word, every struggle, every triumph.

Each article, each interview, each grainy video of actors rehearsing monologues in tiny rented apartments—every piece of it was a whisper in his mind, a voice that told him he wasn't alone. That there were others like him, others who had felt this same longing, others who had taken the leap.

Yet, even as he devoured these stories, the weight of his secret grew heavier.

Every morning, he folded his dream away like an old letter, tucking it into the corners of his mind where no one could find it. He tried to return to his routine—to the endless pages of formulas, to the carefully structured world of numbers and logic. But they felt foreign now, like a language he no longer understood.

His heart wasn't in it.

His mind wasn't in it.

He was supposed to be preparing for IIT, but all he could think about were stage lights. About standing in front of an audience, about losing himself in a character, about speaking words that made people feel something real.

But in his world, dreams like that weren't meant to be spoken aloud.

They were meant to be buried.

The fear of speaking up, of shattering the illusion that had been so carefully built around him, kept him silent. But silence was no longer an option.

The moment of truth was coming.

And deep down, Ashutosh knew—there would be no turning back.

ppp

Some words are easy to say. Others sit heavy in the chest, waiting for the right moment—though deep down, you know that moment will never come.

Ashutosh had rehearsed this conversation a thousand times in his head. He had imagined different versions of it—some where his father listened in silence, some where his mother held his hand, some where the entire house erupted in anger.

But no matter how many times he pictured it, nothing could prepare him for reality.

That evening, as the family gathered for dinner, the weight of unspoken truth settled in his bones. The clatter of plates, the murmur of casual conversation, the scent of freshly cooked dal—it was all familiar, all normal. But inside him, a storm raged.

His younger siblings ate without a care in the world, giggling about school, while his mother quietly served food, her gaze flickering toward him every so often. She knew something was coming. She had sensed it for weeks.

His father, seated at the head of the table, was reading the newspaper between bites, as he always did. Occasionally, he would make a comment about the state of the country, about some student who had secured a top rank, about the competition for IIT seats getting fiercer every year.

"You know," his father said, flipping a page, *"I read about this boy from a small town—ranked first in JEE Advanced. Full scholarship, job offers even before graduation. That could be you, Ashutosh. Just one more year of hard work, and the future is yours."*

Ashutosh tightened his grip on his spoon. His stomach twisted. His heartbeat roared in his ears.

There would never be a perfect moment.

There would never be a time when his father would nod in understanding, when his relatives would applaud his decision, when society would embrace his choice.

So, he simply said it.

"Papa, I don't want to go to IIT."

The words dropped like a stone into still water, shattering the quiet.

His siblings stopped chewing. His mother froze, her hands hovering over the serving bowl.

For a moment, his father didn't react. He simply lowered the newspaper, his eyes sharp, unreadable. *"What did you just say?"*

Ashutosh's throat felt dry, but he forced himself to continue. *"I don't want to be an engineer. I want to go to Mumbai... to study acting."*

The silence that followed was suffocating.

His father's expression didn't change immediately, but something in his eyes did. The quiet pride that had always been there—the certainty of his son's future—wavered, darkened.

His mother was the first to react. *"Ashu, beta... what are you saying?"* Her voice was barely a whisper, as if saying it out loud would make it real.

His siblings looked back and forth between their parents and him, too young to fully grasp what was happening but sensing that something had shifted.

Then, his father spoke.

"You want to throw away everything?" His voice was calm, but it was the kind of calm that came before a storm. *"After all these years? After everything we've given you?"*

"It's not throwing it away, Papa. It's—"

*"It **is** throwing it away!"* His father's voice was suddenly sharp, cutting through the room. *"Do you even understand what you're saying? Do you know what an IIT degree means? What it can do for your life? And you want to give all that up... for what? To **act**?"*

Ashutosh swallowed hard. *"I know what I want."*

His father laughed—a short, humorless laugh. *"You **think** you know what you want. But what you want is foolishness."* He shook his head, anger simmering just beneath the surface. *"You will come to your senses. This conversation is over."*

"No, it's not," Ashutosh said, his voice steady. *"Because I've made my decision."*

His mother placed a trembling hand on his arm. *"Ashu, please. Think about this. You have such a bright future ahead of you—why would you risk it all?"*

"Because this is not my future," he said, his voice cracking despite his resolve. *"This is yours. This is what you all decided for me before I even had a say. But I do have a say. And I choose this."*

His father pushed his plate away. *"Enough."*

His siblings stared at their plates, too scared to move. His mother's eyes shone with unshed tears.

And just as he had expected, the silence that followed was deafening.

It was the sound of a home no longer feeling like home.

ᐻᐻᐻ

His father's disbelief turned to anger. His mother's worry turned to tears. His uncle, who had once boasted about him to the neighbors, shook his head in utter disappointment.

The news spread quickly among relatives, traveling through hushed conversations over phone calls and whispered discussions in the neighborhood. *Ashutosh wants to become an actor.* It was said not with curiosity or encouragement, but with shock and pity, as if he had confessed to a terrible crime.

That night, the house was heavy with tension.

His father sat in his usual chair, his arms crossed, his jaw set tight. His mother stood nearby, wringing the edge of her dupatta between trembling fingers. His uncle leaned against the wall, staring at Ashutosh as if he had suddenly become a stranger.

His father's voice was sharp. *"Say it again. Say it so I know I didn't mishear you the first time."*

"I don't want to go to IIT," Ashutosh repeated, his voice steadier than he felt. *"I want to go to Mumbai. I want to become an actor."*

A muscle twitched in his father's jaw. His hands tightened into fists. *"Do you even understand what you're saying?"* he demanded. *"Do you think this is some joke? Some *hobby*? We have spent years—years—shaping your future, making sure you have every opportunity. And you want to throw it all away for some—some *drama*?"*

His mother wiped at her eyes. *"Beta, please. We are not against you being happy. But acting? It's not practical. It's not secure. You have a bright future waiting for you. Why would you risk everything?"*

*"Because it's not *my* future,"* Ashutosh said, his voice rising despite himself. *"It's yours. It's everyone else's. But it's not mine."*

His uncle scoffed. *"This is what happens when children get too much freedom. They start thinking they can do whatever they want. You are not some Bollywood hero, Ashutosh. You are a small-town boy. Dreams like this? They don't come true for people like us."*

His father pointed a finger at him. *"Enough of this nonsense. You **will** write the entrance exam. You **will** get into IIT. And you **will** become an engineer."*

"No," Ashutosh said, his voice unwavering.

His father's eyes darkened with something beyond anger—disbelief, betrayal. *"What did you say?"*

"No, Papa," he repeated, more firmly this time. *"I won't do it. I won't waste years of my life doing something I don't love. I won't live a life that doesn't feel like mine."*

His mother shook her head. *"Ashu, you don't understand—"*

"I do understand, Maa," he interrupted. *"I understand perfectly. For years, I've done everything right. I've followed every rule, met every expectation. I never complained, never asked for anything. But this—this one thing—I have to do."*

His father exhaled sharply, shaking his head. *"No. Absolutely not. I will not let my son become a nautanki on some stage. This discussion is over."*

But for the first time in his life, Ashutosh did not back down.

The arguments continued for days. Long, exhausting battles that led nowhere. Each conversation ended the same way—with his father storming out, with his mother begging him to reconsider, with his uncle shaking his head in disappointment.

"You are making a mistake," his father warned him.

"If you go down this path, don't expect us to support you," his uncle added.

His mother, her voice thick with unshed tears, whispered, *"Beta, think about your family. Think about what this will do to us."*

But Ashutosh had already spent years thinking about everyone else.

Now, for the first time, he was thinking about himself.

He wanted to act.

He needed to act.

And no matter how much it hurt, no matter how much it cost him, he wasn't going to stop now.

ᐒᐒᐒ

It was his mother who softened first.

She, too, had been raised in a world where dreams were a luxury few could afford. She knew what it meant to sacrifice desire for duty, to silence one's own voice for the sake of family and expectations. But a mother knows her child. And she had seen something in Ashutosh—something his father refused to see.

She had watched him grow up under the weight of responsibility, watched him bury his true self beneath textbooks and equations. But she had also seen the quiet moments when he thought no one was watching—the way his face lit up when he spoke about films, the way his fingers unconsciously traced invisible lines in the air as if performing an unseen scene. There had never been that fire in his eyes when he spoke about engineering.

This was not rebellion. This was not a phase. This was who he was.

And so, one evening, after another long, exhausting argument had faded into silence, she placed a gentle hand on her husband's arm.

"Maybe we should listen to him," she said softly.

Her husband's face was unreadable, his hands clenched into fists on his lap. *"You want me to *listen*? To what? To our son throwing away everything for a foolish dream?"*

She sighed, choosing her words carefully. *"He's never asked for anything before. Never once. Have you ever seen him fight for something like this?"*

He looked away, his jaw tightening. *"That doesn't mean he's right."*

"No," she agreed. *"But it means this matters to him. More than we ever realized."*

Her husband exhaled sharply, shaking his head. *"You think this world is kind to people like us? You think Mumbai is waiting for him with open arms? We are setting him up for failure."*

She hesitated, then spoke the words that had been lingering in her heart.

"If we force him down a path he doesn't want, aren't we setting him up for failure anyway?"

A heavy silence filled the room.

Her husband didn't respond. He didn't agree. But for the first time, he didn't argue either.

And for Ashutosh, that silence was the first crack in the walls that had caged him for so long.

❦❦❦

His father did not agree—not fully. The disappointment lingered in his eyes, heavy and unspoken, filling the spaces between their conversations. It was there in the quiet clatter of dishes at dinner, in the deep sighs that replaced words, in the way he looked at Ashutosh as if searching for the son he thought he knew.

But in the end, he did not stop him.

The night before his departure, his father stood by the doorway of Ashutosh's room, watching him pack. The air was thick with everything they wanted to say but couldn't.

Finally, his father spoke, his voice quieter than usual. *"You've made your choice. Now don't come running back if it doesn't work out."*

Ashutosh's hands stilled over his suitcase. He swallowed, then nodded. *"I won't."*

His father turned away, but before he left, he murmured, almost as an afterthought, *"Keep your mother's number saved. Don't forget to call her."*

And just like that, it was done.

But while the rest of the house carried the weight of disappointment, there was one corner where excitement bloomed.

His sisters were the only ones who had truly, wholeheartedly supported him.

"You're actually doing it!" Rachna, whispered as she helped him fold his clothes. *"You're going to Mumbai, bhai. You're going to be an actor."*

"A *big actor!*" added Neha, her eyes gleaming. *"One day, we'll see you on TV, and we'll tell everyone—that's our bhai!"*

Ashutosh chuckled, ruffling her hair. *"Not so fast. I haven't even stepped foot in Mumbai yet."*

Rachna grinned. *"But you *will*. And you'll make it. I just know it."*

Unlike the others, they did not question him. They did not remind him of what he was leaving behind. They only saw what lay ahead—the dream, the possibilities, the future that he was daring to chase.

As the first rays of morning light filtered through the windows, they stood by the door, watching him get ready to leave.

"Don't forget us when you become famous," Neha teased, though her voice wavered slightly.

"Never," Ashutosh said firmly. *"No matter what happens, I'll always be your bhaiya."*

The station was crowded, the air thick with the smell of chai and rusting metal. As Ashutosh stepped onto the train, his mother held his hand one last time, pressing something into his palm—a small packet of homemade sweets.

"For when you miss home," she said softly.

His father stood a few steps behind, arms crossed, face unreadable. He said nothing, but he was there. And that, perhaps, was enough.

As the train pulled away from Gorakhpur, Ashutosh watched his hometown shrink into the distance, its familiar sights blurring into nothingness. The weight of expectations still clung to him, wrapped around his shoulders like an old, heavy coat.

But for the first time in his life, there was something else.

A new kind of weight. A new kind of fear.

The weight of freedom. The fear of the unknown.

And somewhere within both, the quiet thrill of stepping into a world where he could finally be himself.

4

The City of Dreams

Every dream comes with a price. It is not just about talent or ambition—it is about endurance, about the willingness to stand firm when the world tells you to give up. It is about stepping into the unknown with nothing but belief, knowing that failure is not just possible but inevitable, and choosing to move forward anyway.

Some cities are built to test you. They lure you in with promises, only to push you to your limits, to see if you have what it takes to survive. They do not hand out success easily; they demand sacrifices, patience, and an unwavering will.

Mumbai is one such city. It welcomes dreamers with open arms but does not promise them a smooth road ahead. It is a place where talent is abundant, where ambitions collide, where the thin line between hope and despair is walked every single day. Here, people arrive with nothing but faith in themselves, and many leave with broken spirits, swallowed by the weight of their own aspirations.

But for those who dare to persist, for those who refuse to surrender, this city has the power to transform lives. It can turn nobodies into legends.

For Ashutosh, stepping into Mumbai was not just about chasing a dream. It was about proving—to himself, to his family, to the world—that he was meant for something more. That he could carve a place for himself in a city where millions had tried and failed.

The real test was about to begin.

ᐅᐅᐅ

Mumbai was nothing like Gorakhpur. It wasn't just the size of the city or the towering buildings that made it different—it was the speed at which everything moved. The moment Ashutosh stepped off the train at Chhatrapati Shivaji Terminus, he was engulfed in a wave of noise, movement, and energy unlike anything he had ever known. People rushed past him in all directions, pushing, weaving, shouting, as if the whole city was in a hurry to be somewhere.

The honking of taxis and auto-rickshaws filled the air, mixing with the rhythmic clatter of local trains in the distance. Street vendors shouted over one another, advertising everything from chai to vada pav to cheap mobile covers. A group of men argued in rapid Marathi near the ticket counter, while a family struggled to carry their luggage across the platform.

Ashutosh stood frozen for a moment, gripping the handle of his suitcase. The air smelled different—salty, humid, thick with sweat, spices, and exhaust fumes. It was overwhelming, yet exhilarating.

This was the city where dreams were built. And shattered. And rebuilt again.

A porter, noticing his hesitation, called out, *"Kidhar jaana hai, bhai?" (Where do you wanna go?)*

Ashutosh snapped out of his daze. *"Andheri,"* he said, trying to sound confident. He had rehearsed everything in his mind—where he had to go, the train he had to take, the route he had to follow—but now, standing in the middle of this chaos, he felt small, lost, like an outsider in a world that was already moving without him.

His phone buzzed. It was a message from Rohit.

Reached?

Ashutosh exhaled, tightening his grip on his suitcase.

Yes.

There was no turning back now.

�गᗰᗰ

The first few days in Mumbai felt like a blur, a whirlwind of unfamiliar streets, impatient crowds, and an exhausting search for stability. The city moved too fast, its people too busy, its streets a confusing maze of possibilities and dead ends. There were moments when he felt like he was drowning, swept away by the sheer enormity of it all.

Finding a place to stay had been harder than he had imagined. Rented rooms were expensive, hostels overcrowded, and landlords wary of newcomers—especially those without steady jobs. Every inquiry ended in either a price he couldn't afford or a hesitant shake of the head. *"Actors? No, no, we don't rent to actors. Too unstable."*

Eventually, after days of searching, he found a small room in a crumbling chawl in Andheri, close enough to the acting institute he had enrolled in. It wasn't much. Just four walls, a rusted ceiling fan that groaned with every turn, and a single window that overlooked a narrow, damp alley. The walls were stained from years of neglect, the floor uneven, the air thick with the scent of dampness and dust. But none of that mattered.

Because it was his.

His new home.

Money became his next battle. He had brought what little savings his mother had managed to give him, careful to tuck it away in his suitcase as if it were more precious than gold. But Mumbai devoured money faster than he had expected. Rent, food, travel—everything had a price.

He quickly learned to stretch every rupee. Expensive meals were out of the question, so he found solace in roadside vada pavs, spicy and cheap, the kind that burned his tongue but filled his stomach. Tea stalls became his go-to, their sugary chai giving him just enough energy to get through long days. He avoided auto-rickshaws, opting instead for packed local trains, where he was shoved, squeezed, and pushed against strangers in a battle for space.

His wardrobe, once neatly arranged back in Gorakhpur, was now limited to a handful of clothes, worn and reworn until the fabric lost its crispness. Laundry was done in a bucket, hung to dry by the single window that let in slivers of Mumbai's polluted air.

He had never lived like this before. But he had no complaints.

Every night, exhaustion pulled at his body, but his mind refused to rest. He lay on his narrow cot, staring at the cracked ceiling, reminding himself why he was here. He had come to this city to become something, to prove that his dreams weren't foolish, that he wasn't just another boy with empty ambitions.

There was no room for self-doubt.

This city demanded everything. And he was ready to give it.

⸖⸖⸖

Enrolling in the acting institute was more than just a formality—it was the first step toward turning his dream into something real, something tangible. From the moment Ashutosh stepped inside, he felt the air buzzing with a nervous energy. The institute was filled with hopefuls from every corner of the country, each one carrying their own version of his dream, their own desperation to make it big. Some came from wealthy families, supported by parents who believed in them. Others, like him, had arrived with nothing but passion and the weight of everything they had left behind.

The walls of the institute were covered with faded posters of legends—Dilip Kumar, Amitabh Bachchan, Shah Rukh Khan—men who had once been nobodies in this city, just like them. Their faces stared down at the students as if testing them, as if asking: *Do you have what it takes?*

The lessons were unlike anything he had ever experienced. They weren't about memorizing lines or copying famous performances. No one cared how well he could imitate an actor from an old movie.

"Acting is not about pretending," one of the instructors announced on the first day, pacing across the room. *"It's about truth. You don't act. You become."*

Ashutosh listened carefully, scribbling notes in the last pages of his notebook, the same way he used to write secret dialogues back in school.

They spoke of voice modulation—how a single shift in tone could change the meaning of a line.

They taught him about body language—how a droop of the shoulders could tell a story without words.

They pushed him to explore expressions, emotions, and the silences in between.

And most difficult of all, they asked him to *forget himself.*

"Strip away everything," another instructor told them. *"Forget your name, your past, your fears. You are not Ashutosh Rana from Gorakhpur. You are whoever the scene demands you to be."*

It was harder than he had expected.

Back home, in his tiny room, acting had been simple. He had stood in front of his cracked mirror, mouthing monologues, mimicking his favorite stars, delivering dialogues with the precision of a well-rehearsed script. But here, they wanted something more. They didn't want words. They wanted *truth.*

They wanted him to *feel.*

When given a scene, he couldn't just repeat a line the way it was written. He had to *live* it.

"Think of the moment before the moment," his instructor told him during one session. *"What happened just before your character says this line? What are they feeling? If you don't know that, you're just reciting words."*

Some days, he felt like he was making progress. When he connected with a scene, when his voice cracked with real emotion, when he saw a flicker of approval in his instructor's eyes—those moments made it all feel worth it.

But other days... other days were unbearable.

There were days when he felt lost, when nothing clicked, when he couldn't feel anything at all. Days when his voice felt hollow, when his expressions felt forced, when the self-doubt crept in like a shadow whispering: *Maybe you were never meant for this.*

Some nights, he lay awake in his cramped room, staring at the damp ceiling, wondering if he had made a terrible mistake.

But then he would remind himself—Mumbai had taken everything from him, but it had also given him something no one else ever had.

A chance.

And he wasn't about to waste it.

ᗡᗡᗡ

Mumbai did not welcome dreamers with open arms. It was a city that demanded proof of perseverance before offering even the slightest reward. Every street, every café, every rundown apartment was brimming with people who had arrived with the same hunger, the same desperate hope of making it. Some had been here for months, others for years, but all of them were fighting the same silent battle—to be *seen*, to be *heard*, to be *chosen*.

Ashutosh quickly learned that rejection in this city was not personal. It was mechanical. Cold. Efficient.

He stood in long lines outside casting studios, waiting for his turn, surrounded by dozens of others who looked just like him—young men with well-rehearsed monologues, neatly ironed shirts, and eyes filled with a fragile blend of confidence and fear.

Inside the audition rooms, the process was swift and unsparing. Casting directors barely looked up from their desks, flipping through headshots, dismissing hopefuls with a monotone:

"Next."

"Not the right look."

"Come back when you have experience."

At first, he thought if he just gave his best performance, if he poured his heart into every dialogue, someone would notice. But the truth was harsher—no one had the time. No one cared about effort, only results.

He saw actors—some more talented than him, some less—walk away with roles because of connections, because of luck, because of something that had nothing to do with talent. He saw others, broken by rejection, pack their bags and leave the city forever.

There were days he left auditions feeling invisible, like a ghost drifting through a city that refused to acknowledge his existence. He wanted to scream, to shake someone, to ask if anyone even saw him.

But Mumbai did not stop for anyone's frustration. It moved forward, indifferent to those who couldn't keep up.

Through all of it, his family remained his tether to the world he had left behind.

His sisters called him almost every evening, their voices filled with excitement and hope.

"Bhai, did you meet any famous actors today?" Neha, would ask, her enthusiasm unshaken by reality.

"Not yet," Ashutosh would reply with a small smile, *"but soon."*

"Mummy says she prays for you every day," Rachna, the elder sister, added. *"She tells Papa you'll make us proud."*

Their words were a balm on the wounds Mumbai left behind. They were the only ones who had supported him without hesitation, the only ones who never doubted that he would make it.

His mother's voice, however, carried a quiet worry beneath her encouragement.

"You're eating properly, na? You sound tired."

"I'm fine, Maa. Just busy."

She never pressed, never asked about the struggles she must have sensed. But sometimes, in the pauses between their words, he could hear her sighs, the silent weight of a mother's unspoken fears.

His father rarely spoke to him. Their conversations were brief, formal, distant.

"Doing well?"

"Yes, Papa."

"Hmm."

That was it. No reprimands, no taunts—just silence filled with the weight of expectations he had walked away from.

Every morning, he woke up with renewed determination. Every rejection was a blow, but none strong enough to knock him down completely.

He took up small gigs—background work, student films, anything that could give him a taste of being in front of a camera. They weren't glamorous. Sometimes, he played a man in a crowd. Other times, he had a single line in an independent short film that would never be seen beyond a handful of film school screenings.

But he kept going.

Because this was the path he had chosen.

And no matter how hard the city tried to break him, he wasn't ready to let go just yet.

ᐅᐅᐅ

Months passed, but success still felt like a distant dream. The city had not broken him, but it had not embraced him either. He was stuck somewhere in between—floating in uncertainty, surviving but not thriving, hopeful but exhausted.

His savings were dwindling. The rejections had become so frequent that they no longer stung as sharply, just a dull ache he had learned to live with. Every night, he lay in his tiny room, staring at the cracked ceiling, wondering how much longer he could hold on.

But in the quiet, in the stillness after the chaos of the day, one thought kept him going:

He had not come this far to give up now.

No matter how many doors slammed in his face, no matter how many times he had to start over, he would keep fighting. Because beyond the exhaustion, beyond the fear, beyond the uncertainty—there was still a flicker of something deep inside him.

A dream.

And as long as it was alive, so was he.

5

The Harsh Reality

Dreams often appear golden from a distance, shining with the promise of success and fulfillment. But as one walks closer, the sheen begins to fade, revealing the cracks beneath—the struggle, the sacrifices, the unrelenting hardships that no one speaks about.

Reality does not offer soft landings. It does not hand out success simply because someone dares to dream. Instead, it throws obstacles, demands patience, and tests resilience in ways that few can anticipate. It is not enough to be passionate; one must also be prepared for the loneliness, the exhaustion, the constant battle between hope and despair.

There comes a point when enthusiasm begins to wane, when the initial fire starts flickering under the weight of rejection, uncertainty, and the slow passage of time. This is the moment that defines a dreamer—not the one where they set out full of excitement, but the one where they stand battered by reality and must decide whether to keep going or turn back.

Because dreaming is easy. Enduring is not.

Ashutosh had arrived in Mumbai with a suitcase full of clothes and a heart overflowing with ambition. He had believed that talent would be enough, that if he worked hard, gave his best at every audition, and poured his soul into his craft, the industry would recognize him.

He was wrong.

The city did not function on dreams alone. It ran on connections, persistence, and a cruel hierarchy that no one warned outsiders about. The casting calls were brutal—rooms packed with hopefuls just like him, all reciting the same dialogues, all vying for the same fleeting chance to be seen. The waiting hours were long, the auditions brief, and the rejections immediate. Sometimes, there wasn't even a rejection—just silence, a dismissal without words, a nod toward the door.

At first, he convinced himself that this was part of the process. Everyone faced rejection. He would try again. And again.

But as days turned into weeks, and weeks into months, the weight of it all began to settle on his shoulders.

One afternoon, he found himself standing outside a casting office in Andheri, sweat dripping down his back despite the cool breeze. He had waited for hours, only to be told, *"Sorry, we're looking for someone with experience."*

Experience? How was he supposed to get experience if no one gave him a chance?

He walked away, his feet dragging, his body exhausted. He had skipped lunch to make it on time, spent his last few rupees on a train ticket, and now he had nothing—not even a single line spoken in front of a camera.

That night, lying on his thin mattress in his cramped room, hunger gnawed at his stomach, but a deeper emptiness gnawed at his heart.

For the first time since he had arrived in Mumbai, a thought crept into his mind—one that terrified him more than failure itself.

Was this a mistake?

ÞÞÞ

The audition halls were always packed. The air inside them felt heavy, thick with unspoken desperation. Every morning, Ashutosh found himself standing in yet another endless queue, surrounded by faces just like his—young men with neatly pressed shirts, portfolios in hand, each rehearsing lines under their breath, each praying that today would be *the* day.

But the casting rooms held no sympathy.

When his turn finally came, he would step forward, heart pounding, voice steady.

"Name?" a bored assistant would ask, barely glancing up from a clipboard.

"Ashutosh Rana."

A nod. No eye contact. A pen scratching against paper.

"Height?"

"Five feet ten."

Another nod.

"Profile."

He turned to his left, then to his right, as instructed. A camera clicked. Sometimes, that was all they needed.

"Okay, we'll call you."

Dismissed. Just like that.

Some auditions allowed him to at least perform, to bring life to the lines he had practiced a hundred times over. He poured his emotions into every word, every gesture, hoping—begging silently—that someone would notice, that someone would see *him*, not just another face in the crowd.

But most of the time, they barely looked up.

"Next."

And that was it.

Rejection came in many forms. Sometimes it was polite, sometimes it was cruel.

"You don't have the right look."

"We're looking for someone fairer."

"You don't have the right aura."

What did that even mean?

He tried not to take it personally. He tried to remind himself that this was the industry, that everyone faced rejection, that he just needed to keep going.

But it wasn't easy.

He started recognizing faces—other struggling actors who showed up at every audition, just like him. Some were older, their eyes tired, their enthusiasm dulled by years of waiting. Others were fresh, still holding onto the same naive hope he had carried when he first arrived.

They exchanged nods, brief conversations in between auditions.

"How did it go?" someone would ask.

"Same story."

"They didn't even look at me."

"Bro, I think I'm done. I might head back home next month."

Some of them disappeared after a few months. One day, they were there, waiting in line, practicing their lines. The next, they were gone.

Swallowed by the city's indifference.

Abandoned dreams.

Ashutosh feared he might be next.

But still, he kept going.

ppp

Mumbai was ruthless to those without money. Every day felt like a delicate balancing act, stretching each rupee as far as it would go. There were no luxuries—no casual cups of coffee, no auto rides when he could walk, no meals beyond the cheapest street food stalls.

His savings had dried up faster than he had expected, leaving him scrambling for work wherever he could find it. Some days, he managed to assist at local theaters, running errands for directors, cleaning rehearsal spaces, even helping actors memorize their lines. Other days, he found himself outside bustling railway stations, handing out pamphlets to indifferent passersby.

"Sir, acting classes—first session free!" he would call out, holding out a leaflet.

Most people ignored him. Some took the pamphlet and tossed it aside without a glance. Once, a man smirked at him and said, *"Struggling actor, huh? Good luck with that."*

Luck. He needed more than that.

When there was no work, hunger became a test of endurance. He learned to survive on cutting chai and vada pavs, the cheapest food Mumbai had to offer. Some nights, when money ran out entirely, he drank water until his stomach felt full and willed himself to sleep.

And yet, no matter how bad things got, he refused to call home for help. His father's disappointment still echoed in his mind. *You want to waste your life? Go ahead.* Asking for money would mean admitting failure, and that was something he wasn't ready to do.

There was a time when Ashutosh had been *somebody*. In Gorakhpur, people knew his name. His teachers had praised him, his relatives had boasted about his bright future, his parents had pinned their hopes on him.

But in Mumbai, he was no one. Just another face in the crowd, another struggler chasing an impossible dream.

Nobody cared about his academic achievements, his talent, or his sacrifices. The city didn't stop to acknowledge the boy who had once been the pride of his family. Here, he was just another nameless soul, trying not to be swallowed whole.

The realization stung, but there was no time to dwell on it. Survival didn't allow self-pity.

His tiny room in Andheri, which had once felt like a symbol of freedom, now felt suffocating. The walls were cracked, the ceiling fan creaked through the night, and the smell of dampness clung to everything. The flickering tube light cast long shadows, making the space feel even smaller.

At night, silence pressed down on him. It wasn't the peaceful quiet of home; it was the kind that amplified his doubts, that whispered *Maybe you made a mistake*.

He lay awake, staring at the ceiling, his mind replaying the countless rejections, the indifferent looks, the endless struggles. He had imagined this journey to be hard, but *this*—this constant fight to simply exist—he hadn't been prepared for.

But no matter how heavy the nights felt, when the sun rose, he forced himself to rise with it. Because as much as the city tried to break him, he wasn't ready to give up. Not yet.

ᗰᗰᗰ

Mumbai was always alive—its streets packed with people, its trains bursting with bodies, its nights as restless as its days. And yet, Ashutosh had never felt more alone.

Back home, there had always been voices around him—his father's stern words, his mother's gentle reassurances, his sisters' endless chatter. Even on his worst days, there had been someone to talk to, someone to share a meal with, someone who *cared*.

Here, the only voice he often heard was his own, echoing in the cramped silence of his one-room apartment. The loneliness was suffocating.

His only escape was the phone calls home.

His mother's voice was the first thing he sought after particularly bad days. No matter how exhausted he was, no matter how much disappointment clung to him, hearing her made the weight on his shoulders a little lighter.

"How are you, my son?" she would ask, her voice always soft, always concerned.

"I'm fine, Maa," he would reply, forcing a smile she couldn't see.

She would ask if he was eating properly, if he was taking care of himself. He would lie. He had to. What was the point of making her worry? She already had enough on her mind.

But it was his sisters who made him feel like he hadn't completely disappeared from the world.

Unlike the rest of his family, they had never questioned his decision, never doubted him.

"Bhai, tell us, how was the audition?" his sister would ask, her voice filled with excitement.

"I'm sure you'll get selected this time!" Rachna would add, always the optimist.

They celebrated even his smallest wins—his first callback, his first minor theater role, his first time standing in front of a camera, even if it was just as an extra.

"You two are happier than me," he would joke, trying to match their enthusiasm.

"Of course! One day, when you become a big actor, we'll proudly say—he is our brother!" they would say with absolute confidence.

Their belief in him never wavered. Even when his own confidence cracked, even when he questioned himself, they *believed*.

But there were things he didn't tell them.

He didn't tell them about the nights he sat in front of the mirror, staring at his reflection, whispering lines over and over again until they sounded meaningless. He didn't tell them about the casting directors who didn't even bother to look up from their phones when they rejected him. He didn't tell them about the nights he went to bed hungry, too broke to afford dinner.

His mother always ended their calls the same way.

"Son, if it ever gets too difficult, come home."

He never said yes. He never said no.

Because going back meant admitting he had failed. And he wasn't ready to do that.

Not yet.

ᛈᛈᛈ

The months stretched into a blur of rejection, exhaustion, and an unshakable sense of invisibility. Mumbai had a cruel way of welcoming dreamers—offering glimpses of hope before snatching them away, testing just how much disappointment one could endure before breaking.

Ashutosh had once walked into auditions with confidence, believing that his passion alone would set him apart. But he had learned the harsh truth. Talent was not enough. Passion was not enough.

And so, he watched.

He watched newcomers arrive, their eyes alight with ambition, their voices brimming with certainty—*This is it. This is where it all begins.*

He had been like them once.

But as weeks passed, he saw the same faces lose their shine. The endless auditions, the constant rejection, the cruel indifference of the city—it all wore them down. One by one, they disappeared, leaving behind only a handful who still clung to their fragile dreams.

And every time someone left, he wondered—*How much longer before I become one of them?*

Doubt became a constant companion, creeping into his mind in the quiet hours of the night.

"What if I was never meant for this?"

"What if I'm just another fool chasing an illusion?"

"What if I already threw away my only real chance at a future?"

The questions gnawed at him, relentless and unkind. There were nights he lay awake, staring at the cracked ceiling of his tiny room, feeling as though the city itself was closing in on him, waiting for him to surrender.

The weight of failure pressed down on his shoulders, heavier with each passing day.

And yet... he couldn't leave.

Despite everything, despite the rejection, the loneliness, the hunger—something inside him refused to die.

The dream still lived, flickering like a candle in a storm, fragile but unyielding.

There were moments—brief, fleeting moments—when he would stand in front of a mirror, reciting lines with the same fire he had felt as a boy in Gorakhpur. Moments when he would watch a great performance on screen and feel the same rush, the same longing, the same *need* to be up there.

Moments when he knew, deep in his soul, that he couldn't walk away.

Not yet.

But dreams, he was learning, came at a cost.

And he was beginning to wonder if he had the strength to keep paying the price.

ᐅᐅᐅ

Mumbai did not wait for anyone. The city kept moving, indifferent to those who faltered, ruthless to those who hesitated. It chewed up dreamers and spit them out without a second thought.

And yet, Ashutosh remained.

He woke up every morning with the same hunger, the same unshaken resolve, even as exhaustion weighed heavy on his bones. He pushed himself into every audition, every side job, every fleeting opportunity, because stopping meant surrendering, and he wasn't ready for that. Not yet.

But as another day ended, as he walked back to his tiny room under flickering streetlights, a quiet fear settled in his chest.

How long can I keep this up?

How much more can I take before the city breaks me, too?

He didn't have the answers.

All he knew was that tomorrow, the struggle would begin again. The doors would remain closed, the rejections would pile up, and the world would continue to look past him.

But he would show up anyway.

Because as long as he was still standing, as long as even a shred of his dream remained—there was still a chance.

And for now, that had to be enough.

6

First Sip of Escape

Everyone searches for an escape. Some find it in books, in music, in long walks under city lights. Others find it in silence, in sleep, in the fleeting comfort of distraction. But when reality becomes too heavy—when dreams slip further away and failures pile up—escape takes a different form.

Not all escapes are harmless. Some start as a moment of relief, a brief departure from pain. But before you know it, they turn into something more—a habit, a dependency, a slow unraveling.

Ashutosh wasn't looking for an escape. But when he found one, he didn't let go. Or maybe, it didn't let go of him.

ÞÞÞ

There are moments when the weight of life becomes unbearable. When dreams seem just out of reach, and the effort to chase them feels like running in circles. When every step forward is met with a force pulling you two steps back.

When the city whispers in your ear, *You are not enough.*

When the mirror reflects not just your face, but the exhaustion in your eyes, the lines of stress deepening with each passing day.

In those moments, people search for a way out—a temporary escape, a way to numb the pain, even if just for a little while. Some take refuge in sleep, hoping to dream of a life where things are easier. Others lose themselves in distractions—music, movies, aimless walks through unfamiliar streets.

For Ashutosh, it began with a single drink.

It was not planned. It was not something he had thought about. It was just a night like any other—another failed audition, another day spent running errands for a casting agent who barely remembered his name. His pockets were almost empty, his stomach grumbling in protest after yet another day of stretching his meals too thin. The city felt colder than usual, its lights glaring down at him as if mocking his struggle.

And then came the invitation.

A group of struggling actors he had met at the acting institute called him over. They were sitting outside a dimly lit bar, their laughter cutting through the heavy air of disappointment that always lingered after auditions. Their expressions were a mix of frustration and defiance, as if daring life to break them.

"Come on, Ashu," one of them said, holding up a glass. *"You look like you need this."*

He hesitated. He had never been much of a drinker. Back home, alcohol had always been spoken about in hushed tones, something associated with failure, with lost men who had given up. His father would never forgive him if he knew.

But Mumbai was different. Here, failure had a different scent. It smelled of sweat and cheap cologne, of desperation and cigarette smoke curling in the air. It clung to every struggling artist who had given everything to this city and still found themselves empty-handed.

Ashutosh sat down.

The glass was placed in front of him—a small, amber-colored pool of liquid that seemed harmless enough. The others raised their drinks, toasting to *something*, though no one said exactly what. Maybe to another day survived. Maybe to the hope that tomorrow would be better.

He picked up the glass.

It was just one drink. Nothing more. Just a moment of escape.

ᗡᗡᗡ

The first time Ashutosh drank, it wasn't because he wanted to. It was because he needed something—anything—to quiet the storm inside his head.

The day had been a disaster.

Another audition, another rejection.

He had barely stepped into the room when the casting director, a man who didn't even bother to look up from his phone, waved him off with a curt, "*Next.*"

No feedback. No second chance. Just another door closing in his face.

He had stood there for a second longer than necessary, hoping—praying—that the man would change his mind, that he would look up, really *see* him. But the assistant at the door nudged him out, already calling in the next hopeful, someone taller, sharper, more confident.

And just like that, it was over.

By the time he walked out onto the bustling streets of Mumbai, the weight on his chest was unbearable. The city, always loud, always restless, suddenly felt suffocating. The honking cars, the shouting vendors, the flashing neon lights—it was too much.

He needed to breathe. He needed to stop thinking.

That was how he ended up there—on the cracked pavement outside a small liquor shop in a nameless alleyway, sitting with a few familiar faces from his acting institute. They were all strugglers like him, all carrying the same exhaustion in their eyes.

A half-empty bottle of whiskey sat between them, its glass smudged with fingerprints, passed from one tired dreamer to another.

"Rough day?" someone asked, though it wasn't really a question. They all knew. Every day was rough.

Ashutosh sighed, running a hand through his hair. He didn't respond. He didn't need to.

One of the guys, an actor who had been in Mumbai a few years longer, held out the bottle with a lopsided grin.

"Come on, Ashu. One sip won't kill you."

He hesitated.

Back home, drinking was something *other* men did—men who had lost their way, men who had given up. His father's voice echoed in his head, sharp and disapproving. *"Nothing good ever comes from this."*

But what had come from staying sober? What had come from all his discipline, his sacrifices?

Nothing.

So before he could overthink it, before his conscience could talk him out of it, he grabbed the bottle and took a long sip.

The alcohol burned, sharp and unforgiving, searing down his throat like fire. He coughed, his eyes watering as laughter erupted around him. Someone clapped him on the back.

But as the burn faded, a warmth spread through his chest—slow, comforting. The tension in his shoulders loosened. The self-doubt, the frustration, the sting of rejection—all of it dulled, blurred at the edges.

For the first time in a long while, he wasn't thinking. He wasn't obsessing over auditions, over rent, over what his father would say if he knew.

For the first time, he felt... free.

The night unraveled in a haze of cheap whiskey and aimless conversation. They laughed about things that weren't really funny, cracked jokes about their failures as if they didn't sting. Someone started singing an old Bollywood song off-key, and instead of cringing, Ashutosh found himself joining in, his voice rising above the city's endless noise.

When he finally stumbled back to his cramped room, the floor tilted beneath him, but he didn't care.

For the first time in months, he collapsed onto his bed and slept without tossing, without turning, without waking up in a cold sweat.

The next morning, his head throbbed, his mouth dry as sandpaper. Reality returned, sharper than ever.

But now, he knew a way to make it disappear.

ꕥꕥꕥ

At first, it was harmless.

A drink after an especially bad audition. A few sips after a long, exhausting day at the acting institute. A way to take the edge off when his failures felt too heavy to carry.

"A little won't hurt," he told himself.
"Just today."
"I deserve it after the day I've had."
And he did.
Didn't he?
One drink turned into two. Two turned into three.

At first, he only drank with friends. The same group of strugglers who had introduced him to that first sip. It was easy to justify when they were all in it together, sitting on crumbling sidewalks, sharing cheap liquor like it was some sacred ritual of the defeated. They weren't drinking to celebrate—they were drinking to forget.

But then, he started drinking alone.

It happened gradually. A night when no one else was free, but the craving was still there. A bottle purchased with the last of his pocket change, hidden away in his room.

The first time, he poured himself just one glass. Just enough to help him sleep.

The second time, he didn't bother with the glass—just took the bottle to his lips and let the burn wash over him.

It was no longer just about dulling the pain. It became part of his routine.

A familiar companion on nights when the loneliness was unbearable.

A way to silence the gnawing fear that maybe, just maybe, he wasn't good enough.

One evening, after another rejection, he sat in his dimly lit room, staring at his reflection in the cracked mirror. His face looked different—tired, older somehow. His eyes lacked the fire they once had.

He uncapped the bottle on his table, the amber liquid catching the weak glow of the flickering bulb above him.

Without thinking, he took a long sip.

The warmth spread through his veins, numbing the ache, dulling the voices in his head that whispered—*"You're wasting your time. You're never going to make it."*

He leaned back against the cold wall, staring at the ceiling. The city outside was alive—horns blaring, people shouting, trains rattling in the distance. But inside this room, everything was still.

He liked that.

The city had started to wear him down.

And alcohol had become his armor.

ᐅᐅᐅ

The changes crept in quietly, like shadows stretching across his life.

At first, they were barely noticeable.

He started showing up late to his acting classes, dragging himself through the doors just as sessions began, sometimes reeking faintly of alcohol from the night before. His instructors gave him questioning looks but said nothing—at least not yet.

Then, he started missing auditions. At first, it was just one or two. *What difference would it make?* There would always be another casting call, another chance. But the missed opportunities began stacking up, one after another, until he wasn't even keeping track anymore.

Even when he did make it to auditions, something was missing. His performances, once electric with passion and hunger, started losing their spark. The fire in his eyes had dulled. The words he spoke felt empty, disconnected from the emotions they were meant to carry.

His teachers noticed.

"You seem distracted, Ashutosh," one of them said after a particularly lifeless monologue reading. Their voice wasn't

harsh, but there was something in their tone—disappointment, maybe. Concern.

"I'm fine," he muttered, forcing a smile.

His friends noticed too.

"Are you okay, Ashu?" someone asked one evening as they gathered outside a tea stall.

He laughed it off. *"Of course. Just tired."*

And he *was* tired. But not in the way they thought.

It wasn't just exhaustion from running between auditions, from juggling classes and survival jobs. It was deeper than that—a bone-deep weariness, the kind that settled into his soul and refused to leave.

The problem with seeking escape is that the real world never stops moving.

The missed auditions added up. The late nights bled into exhausted mornings. The weight of failure still existed—it had just been pushed aside for a while, waiting to crash down on him all at once.

And it did.

One night, after yet another rejection—this one particularly brutal—he sat alone in his dimly lit room. The script for an upcoming audition lay untouched on the table, its crisp pages now meaningless. Beside it, a half-empty bottle rested in his hand.

The silence was deafening.

He could hear the hum of the ceiling fan, the distant honking of cars, the faint laughter of people on the streets below. The city, as always, was alive. But inside his four walls, everything felt suffocatingly still.

He thought about his family.

His mother, who still called every week, her voice laced with concern no matter how much he tried to sound okay.

His sisters, who had always believed in him. Who had dreamed alongside him, waiting for the day he'd tell them he had *finally* made it.

What would they say if they saw him now?

Would they recognize him?

Did *he* even recognize himself anymore?

He stared at the bottle in his hand, turning it slowly, watching the liquid swirl inside.

Somewhere deep down, he knew this wasn't the escape he had been looking for.

But it was the only one he had.

ppp

The first sip had been a choice. A moment of defiance. A single night to quiet the relentless voices in his head. The second had been a habit. A way to soften the sharp edges of disappointment, to turn rejection into something he could swallow.

Now, it was something else entirely.

He wasn't drinking to celebrate. He wasn't drinking to relax.

He was drinking because he didn't know how to *not* drink anymore.

The pattern had settled into his life without him even realizing it. One drink to take the edge off before an audition. Another after, regardless of the outcome. A few sips to help him sleep, to make the silence of his empty room bearable. Before long, the bottle was always there—an unspoken presence in the corner, waiting for him at the end of every exhausting day.

He told himself he was still in control.

I can stop whenever I want.

But the truth was, he never tried.

One evening, after another day of nothing—no callbacks, no opportunities, no hope—Ashutosh sat on the floor of his cramped Andheri room, a half-empty bottle beside him. The fan overhead spun lazily, stirring the humid air, but it did nothing to ease the restlessness in his chest.

His phone buzzed.

He glanced at the screen. His mother.

For a moment, he hesitated. He hadn't spoken to her in days. He knew what she would say. The same quiet concern in her voice, the same unspoken plea hidden behind her words.

"Are you okay?"

"Are you eating properly?"

"Beta, if it gets too hard, come home."

He let the call ring out. He wasn't ready to answer. Not like this.

Instead, he reached for the bottle, tipping it back, feeling the familiar burn slide down his throat.

His father's voice rang in his head, clear despite the alcohol fogging his mind.

"If you waste this opportunity, don't expect to come back."

His grip tightened around the bottle.

He wasn't ready to go back. Not as a failure. Not as someone who couldn't even survive, let alone succeed.

But he wasn't sure how much longer he could keep moving forward either.

His reflection stared back at him from the cracked mirror across the room—hollow eyes, unshaven face, shoulders slumped under the weight of his own choices.

The bottle in his hand felt heavier than ever.

And for the first time, he wondered if this escape wasn't just temporary anymore.

If it had already become his reality.

ppp

The room was silent except for the distant hum of the city outside—cars honking, voices blending, life moving forward while he remained still. The bottle sat beside him, almost empty, its weight no longer just physical but something heavier, something suffocating.

Ashutosh ran a hand over his face, his fingers grazing the rough stubble that had grown unchecked. The mirror across the room reflected someone he barely recognized. The fire in his eyes—the same fire that had once defied his father's wishes, that had burned through his every audition, every struggle—was flickering, struggling against the shadows creeping in.

How had he gotten here?

When had the dream become this?

He closed his eyes, pressing his palms against his temples as if trying to squeeze out the thoughts, the doubts, the gnawing realization that he was slipping. That every night like this was another step further from the Ashutosh Rana who had arrived in Mumbai with nothing but hope and hunger.

The phone buzzed again. He didn't need to look to know who it was.

His mother. His sisters.

People who still believed in him.

He reached for the phone but stopped just short of answering. He couldn't bring himself to hear their voices, to face their concern, to be reminded of the person they thought he still was.

Not yet.

Instead, he reached for the bottle, staring at it for a long moment. Then, with a slow, tired breath, he set it down.

The night stretched before him, silent and heavy.

For the first time, he wasn't sure if he would wake up tomorrow feeling any different.

For the first time, he wasn't sure if he wanted to.

7
A Life of Excess

At first, it feels like control. A conscious choice. A decision to unwind, to loosen the knots of frustration coiled tightly around the mind. It's just a drink after a bad day—something to take the edge off. A rare indulgence. A harmless relief.

But indulgence is deceptive. It doesn't announce itself when it turns into dependency. It moves quietly, inching into daily routine, whispering in moments of weakness. *One more won't hurt. Just tonight. Just this once.* The words come easily, slipping past reasoning like a well-rehearsed script.

And then, without warning, the lines blur.

The drink that was once a weekend escape becomes a nightly ritual. The late nights that started as an exception turn into the norm. Responsibilities shift. Priorities change. What once felt urgent—ambitions, dreams, discipline—start to fade into the background, no longer burning with the same intensity.

It doesn't happen all at once. It's a slow unraveling.

You stop waking up with a purpose. The things that once excited you now feel like burdens. You tell yourself you're fine, that you're still in control. But in reality, you're drifting.

The worst part?

You don't even realize you're falling—until you've already hit the ground. And by then, the way back feels impossibly far.

ᔭᔭᔭ

The change didn't happen overnight. It never does. It was slow, creeping, almost unnoticeable—until it was too late.

What had once been an occasional drink to take the edge off a bad day had now become routine. Auditions, acting classes, and the struggle of making it in the industry had once been at the center of his world. Now, they were afterthoughts, things he would *"get to eventually."* The real world felt too exhausting, too demanding, too full of rejection. But the nights? The nights welcomed him with open arms.

The city transformed after dark. The harshness of the day—the endless waiting in audition lines, the dismissive looks from casting directors, the sinking disappointment of another lost opportunity—faded under neon lights. The bass of the music in the clubs drowned out the self-doubt. The sting of rejection was softened by the burn of whiskey down his throat. And in those moments, he felt invincible, untouchable, free.

But freedom had a price.

It started with invitations.

"You're always so tense, Ashu," a fellow struggler told him one evening after an acting class. *"Come out with us tonight. Forget all this for a while."*

At first, he resisted. *"I have an early audition tomorrow."*

A smirk. A shrug. *"There will always be another audition. But you? You need to live a little."*

That night, he went. And he liked it.

One night turned into two. Then a week. Then longer.

The city's nightlife embraced him, made him feel like he belonged. The dim glow of club lights, the haze of cigarette smoke curling in the air, the pulsating energy of a crowd moving as one—it was a world where no one cared who you were or where you came from. It didn't matter that he was just another struggling actor from Gorakhpur. Here, he was *somebody*—even if just for a few hours.

But the mornings were different.

He woke up with pounding headaches, missed calls from casting agents, and unread messages from his sisters. The scripts he was supposed to study gathered dust on his cluttered desk.

His mother's voice on the phone grew more concerned.

"You sound tired," she said one evening. *"Are you taking care of yourself?"*

He forced a laugh. *"Of course, Ma. Just busy."*

"Busy is good," she said softly. *"But don't lose yourself in it."*

Lose himself.

The words lingered long after the call ended, long after he found himself staring at his reflection in the cracked mirror above his sink. His face was different now—darker circles under his eyes, a hollowness that hadn't been there before.

But the thought didn't stay for long.

Because the next night, the music was loud again. The drinks flowed easily. And the reality of his crumbling ambition faded, just like always.

The auditions started slipping away. He'd forget about them, wake up too late, or show up unprepared. His once-promising performances became lackluster, drained of the passion that had once set him apart.

His teachers at the institute noticed.

"You're distracted, Ashutosh," one of them told him after a particularly lifeless monologue reading. *"This isn't you."*

But maybe it was. Maybe this was who he was now.

The excuses were easy. *I'll get back on track next week. Just one more night out. Just one more drink.*

And yet, each night blurred into the next. Each morning felt heavier than the last.

The dream that had once been his entire world was still there—but it was buried now, beneath hangovers, missed opportunities, and an endless cycle of distraction.

And deep down, he knew it.

He just wasn't sure if he still cared.

ᐁᐁᐁ

Mumbai never slept, and neither did he.

The city had its own rhythm—one that pulsed through the streets long after the sun had set, a beat that never slowed, never waited. Ashutosh had once fought against it, holding onto his dreams, his discipline, his purpose. But now, he found himself moving with it, surrendering to the current that swept him deeper into the night.

The once-occasional drinks had turned into regular outings. What had started as an escape had transformed into a craving—not just for alcohol, but for the night itself.

The auditions, the stress, the failures—none of it mattered when he was bathed in the glow of neon lights, lost in the haze of a crowded bar, his body swaying to music that drowned out every doubt, every disappointment.

Each night was different, yet the same.

One evening, it was a sleek rooftop bar overlooking the city, where laughter mixed with the clinking of glasses and the sky stretched endlessly above them. Another night, it was a dimly lit underground club, where bodies pressed together in a feverish rhythm, and the air was thick with smoke and secrets.

Then there were the house parties—sprawling apartments filled with strangers, bottles scattered across tables, the sound of half-finished conversations blending into the distant hum of a city that never stopped moving.

Here, no one asked where he was from. No one cared about the struggles he carried, the auditions he had failed, or the dreams he had once spoken of with fire in his eyes.

The only thing that mattered was the present—the next drink, the next song, the next distraction.

And Ashutosh, tired of fighting, let himself fall into step with them.

"Another round?" someone would ask, and before he could think, his glass would be full again.

"Live a little, man," a friend would say, laughing as they pulled him onto the dance floor.

And he did.

The faces around him blurred into one another, their voices dissolving into meaningless background noise. He no longer needed to pretend, to put on a show, to prove his worth. In this world, no one expected anything from him.

It was easier this way.

He didn't have to think about the script he hadn't learned, the audition he had missed, or the call from his mother that he had let go unanswered.

The future didn't exist. The past didn't matter.

There was only this—this night, this drink, this fleeting moment of forgetting.

And for now, that was enough.

☙☙☙

The film industry moved forward like an unstoppable machine—directors, producers, casting agents, and actors all chasing their next big break. The city was alive with opportunity. Auditions were happening every day. Roles were being filled. Dreams were being realized.

But Ashutosh wasn't moving anymore.

His world had begun to blur at the edges. Where once his mornings had started with rehearsals, with practice in front of a mirror, with reading scripts and perfecting his craft, now they started with a pounding headache, a dry mouth, and a desperate search for water. The nights had taken over. The drinking, the parties, the endless cycle of escape—it had consumed him.

His phone buzzed constantly with missed calls and unread messages.

A casting director wants to see you tomorrow at 10 AM.

Bro, are you coming to class? Haven't seen you in days.

Ashu, Mom has been calling you. Pick up.

He would stare at the screen, rubbing his temples, his mind foggy from the previous night's drinking. Sometimes he would type out a response and delete it. Other times, he would toss the phone aside and go back to sleep, pushing reality away for just a little longer.

The days blended into nights, and the nights into an endless haze. He barely noticed time slipping through his fingers.

When he did show up for an audition, he wasn't the same Ashutosh who had once stood in front of casting directors with fire in his eyes.

His scripts were untouched, his lines unpracticed. He would mumble through them, his voice lacking conviction, his expressions hollow. His once-sharp instincts had dulled, buried beneath layers of exhaustion and indifference.

The casting directors noticed.

"Thank you. We'll let you know," they would say with a polite nod, already looking toward the next hopeful actor in line.

He wasn't stupid. He knew what that meant. He had once stood on the other side, watching others get dismissed just as quickly.

He had become one of them—the ones who came in, went through the motions, and left without leaving an impression.

And yet, he didn't feel the sharp sting of rejection like he once had.

The first few rejections in Mumbai had hurt like open wounds, gnawing at his confidence, making him question everything. But now?

Now, he barely felt them.

Not because he had grown stronger, but because he had grown numb.

At first, it felt like a relief.

There was no more gut-wrenching disappointment. No more sleepless nights agonizing over what he could have done better. The pain had been replaced with an emptiness that was easier to carry.

But it wasn't relief.

It was surrender.

And deep down, Ashutosh knew it.

ᆑᆑᆑ

Ashutosh's room in Andheri, once a space where he had dreamed, planned, and prepared for his future, had transformed into something unrecognizable. The floor was littered with empty bottles, their labels peeling from condensation and neglect. Clothes—some barely worn, others stained with the remnants of nights he barely remembered—were thrown haphazardly across the room. Scripts, the very things that had once held his purpose, lay scattered and unopened, their pages gathering dust.

The air was stale, thick with the scent of alcohol, sweat, and something unwashed. The flickering tube light cast weak shadows, barely illuminating the chaos. The tiny window that once let in the golden glow of Mumbai's mornings was now covered with a makeshift curtain—a shirt he had tossed there weeks ago, blocking out the sunlight, blocking out the world.

It was as if the room itself had given up.

Just like him.

Ashutosh stood in front of the cracked mirror, his fingers gripping the edges of the rusting sink. He barely recognized the reflection staring back at him. His cheekbones were sharper, not in a sculpted way but in a hollow, tired way. Dark circles hung under his eyes, deep and unshakable. His once-bright gaze, the one that had carried hope and ambition, now looked dull, lifeless.

His fingers ran through his unkempt hair, longer than he usually kept it, greasy from neglect. His skin had lost its glow, replaced with a pale exhaustion that no amount of rest—had he even been resting?—could fix.

He exhaled sharply, gripping the sink tighter. His hands were trembling.

Was it exhaustion?

Or was it the alcohol?

Mumbai, the city he had once seen as a battlefield—one he had been ready to fight in, to carve out his place—now felt like a blur. The towering buildings, the endless streets, the neon lights, and the waves of people rushing towards their ambitions, their goals—it all moved around him, indifferent, uncaring.

He had once walked these streets with determination, rehearsing lines in his head as he made his way to auditions, dreaming of his big break. Now, he wandered them aimlessly, often in a daze, sometimes not even knowing how he had gotten from one place to another.

The city hadn't changed.

He had.

The voice in the back of his head—the one that had been growing quieter with each passing day—tried one last time.

You're losing yourself.

This isn't what you came here for.

Stop. Before it's too late.

For a moment, he considered it. He considered throwing the bottles out, wiping the dust off his scripts, calling his mother, his sisters, and telling them he was going to try again. That he hadn't given up.

But then, his eyes fell on the bottle next to his bed.

Half-full.

Easier.

He grabbed it, twisted off the cap, and poured himself another drink.

The warmth of the alcohol burned his throat, numbing everything else.

Reality could wait.

Tonight, he didn't want to feel.

ッッッ

The bottle tilted in his hand, the amber liquid swirling before slipping past his lips. The burn was familiar now, comforting in a way it shouldn't have been. He leaned back against the wall, staring at the ceiling, at the cracks forming in the plaster—small, almost invisible, but there. Spreading. Just like him.

A part of him knew.

Knew that he was slipping. Knew that this wasn't who he was supposed to be. Knew that every drink he took, every audition he missed, every night lost to neon lights and forgettable faces—was pulling him further from the reason he had come to this city in the first place.

But another part of him—the one that was tired, the one that was afraid—told him it didn't matter. That maybe, this was easier. That maybe, this was who he was now.

The bottle slipped from his fingers, hitting the floor with a dull thud, rolling lazily before coming to a stop. He watched it for a moment, his vision blurring, his mind teetering between awareness and oblivion.

Somewhere in the distance, his phone buzzed.

A call. A message.

Someone trying to reach him.

Someone who still believed he could be saved.

He closed his eyes.

And let the night swallow him whole.

8
The Spiral Downwards

Addiction doesn't come like a storm. It doesn't tear through life in one violent sweep, leaving devastation in its wake. If it did, maybe people would recognize it sooner—maybe they would run before it was too late.

But addiction is quieter. Slower. More insidious.

It arrives like a whisper, slipping into the cracks of exhaustion and despair, offering relief where there is none. It wears the face of comfort, of control, of something you believe you *choose.* A drink to take the edge off. A night out to escape the pressure. A pill to silence the chaos in your mind.

At first, it's occasional, manageable. You tell yourself you have control. That you can stop whenever you want. That you're just *coping.*

But then, something shifts.

It's no longer just about relief—it's about need. The escape isn't temporary anymore. It becomes routine, a crutch, a way of existing. And before you even realize it, the line between indulgence and dependency is gone.

For Ashutosh, the descent had been gradual, slow enough that he had convinced himself it wasn't happening.

He had told himself he was fine, that he still had time, that the dream was still within reach.

But now, he was past the point of falling.

He was crashing.

⮞⮞⮞

Mumbai's nights had always been alive—pulsing with neon lights, the hum of restless voices, the distant thump of music spilling out of bars and clubs. But for Ashutosh, the city's nightlife had transformed into something else entirely. It wasn't about fun anymore. It wasn't about blowing off steam after a tough day.

It was about escape.

And alcohol alone wasn't enough.

It started with a pill. A small, white tablet, casually offered at a party in some dimly lit apartment where the air was thick with cigarette smoke and the scent of expensive cologne.

"This will take the edge off," someone had told him, pressing it into his palm. *"Just try it."*

He had hesitated—only for a second—before placing it on his tongue and washing it down with a sip of whiskey. The bitterness lingered, but then, something shifted.

His body felt lighter. The world slowed down. The worries, the self-doubt, the crushing weight of failure—it all faded into a distant blur.

For the first time in a long time, he felt *free.*

And that feeling?

It was intoxicating.

One time turned into two. Then three. Then so often that he stopped keeping count.

Pills. Powders. Smoke. Whatever dulled the noise in his head, whatever carried him further from the truth he wasn't ready to face.

At first, he told himself it was occasional, something he could control.

I can stop whenever I want.

But addiction doesn't work that way. The body craves more. The mind demands it.

One pill wasn't enough anymore. One drink didn't drown out the thoughts like it used to. His tolerance built up, and soon, he found himself chasing the next high before the last had even worn off.

The nights became longer. The days shorter.

Mornings were lost to pounding headaches, trembling hands, and an empty stomach that rejected anything except the poison he fed it. His body, once strong and resilient, had begun to betray him—his skin looked dull, his frame thinner, his eyes sunken and hollow.

But he ignored it.

Because stopping meant feeling.

And he wasn't ready for that.

ϷϷϷ

Auditions still happened. Roles were still being cast. Mumbai's film industry never stopped moving. But Ashutosh had fallen out of step.

Days blurred together, indistinguishable from one another. Mornings bled into afternoons, afternoons faded into nights, and nights dissolved into hazy, intoxicated voids. Time lost its meaning. He would wake up to missed calls, unread messages, and vague memories of plans he had made but never followed through on.

Casting calls that once sent adrenaline rushing through his veins became nothing more than notifications on his phone—notifications he often ignored.

Until, one day, they simply stopped coming.

The rare times he did manage to drag himself to an audition, he was a shadow of his former self. Gone was the boy who had arrived in Mumbai with fire in his eyes and determination in his heart. Now, he stood before casting directors, unfocused, unprepared, his voice flat, his movements sluggish.

Once, he had poured himself into every role, shaping characters with intensity and raw emotion. Now, he stumbled through lines he hadn't bothered to memorize, his delivery dull, lifeless.

Directors exchanged silent glances. Assistants took notes that no longer mattered.

They had seen this before.

Another struggler who had burned out before even catching fire. Another dreamer swallowed whole by the city's indifference.

It wasn't long before the polite rejections disappeared altogether.

No callbacks. No feedback. No second chances.

The industry had moved on.

The realization didn't hit him all at once. It seeped in slowly, like ink bleeding through paper, darkening everything.

One evening, he scrolled through social media, his bloodshot eyes scanning through posts of familiar faces—actors he had once auditioned alongside, some he had even beaten for roles in the past. They were working, thriving, announcing projects, sharing glimpses from sets he would never step foot on.

And him?

He was sitting in his cluttered room, a half-empty bottle on the floor, his phone screen glowing in the dim light, his name missing from every conversation that mattered.

For the first time, he felt what it was like to be *forgotten.*

༄༄༄

Money had never been abundant. But now, it was disappearing faster than ever, slipping through Ashutosh's fingers like sand.

The occasional gig—helping out at a small theater, running errands for a casting assistant, or a rare role in a student short film—had once been enough to scrape by. He had learned how to stretch every rupee, how to make a single meal last an entire day, how to survive in a city that never made survival easy.

But now, money wasn't being spent on survival. It was being poured into bottles, burned away in smoke-filled rooms, exchanged in dark corners for tiny packets that promised momentary escape.

Rent, food, and travel—the things that had once been priorities—became afterthoughts. If he had enough for another drink, another high, that was all that mattered.

At first, he borrowed from friends.

"Just a little, bhai. I swear, I'll return it next week."

Small amounts. Just enough to get him through the night. And at first, his friends obliged. They were all strugglers, all dreamers trying to carve out their place in the city, and they had all leaned on each other at some point.

But debts have a way of growing, of multiplying.

The amounts got bigger. The promises got emptier.

"Ashu, you still haven't given me back the last two thousand."

"Arre, I'll pay you next week. Just need a little more, yaar. You know how things are."

He meant it. At least, in the moment, he believed he did. But next week came and went, and so did the week after that.

Soon, the same friends who once partied with him, who had laughed at his jokes and poured him drinks, began to avoid him. Messages went unanswered. Calls were met with cold excuses.

"Bhai, I don't have anything to spare right now."

"Sorry, Ashu, I'm tight on cash myself."

Or worse—silence.

The first time he realized a friend had changed the subject the moment he walked into a room, it stung. The tenth time, he didn't even notice anymore.

The landlord's patience wore thinner by the day.

Ashutosh had always been late on rent, but now, the delays stretched into months. The first few times, he had managed to smooth things over with promises.

"Bas ek hafta aur, bhaiya. I have some money coming in."

Then, when that excuse ran dry—

"My account's stuck, technical issues. Just a few more days."

But landlords in Mumbai had seen it all. His tricks didn't work forever. The first warning had been firm but polite. The second had been less forgiving.

And then, one morning, a notice slipped under his door.

FINAL NOTICE: EVICTION IF DUES ARE NOT CLEARED IMMEDIATELY.

The paper felt heavier than it should have. He read it once. Twice. Then crumpled it and tossed it into the mess on his floor.

His rent was overdue. His debts were piling up. He was running out of options.

And yet, when night fell, he still found himself at the same bars, in the same smoke-filled rooms, reaching for the same escape.

Because consequences felt distant.

Because as long as he could get through the *now*, tomorrow could wait.

ppp

Addiction has a way of convincing a person they are alone. That no one understands. That no one cares.

At first, Ashutosh hadn't noticed the shift. The way the calls grew less frequent. The way plans were made without him. The way the people who once felt like family slowly began to drift away.

It started subtly. Excuses from friends when he reached out.

"Bhai, I'm a little busy today. Maybe next time?"

"Got an early morning tomorrow, yaar. You guys enjoy."

And then, the excuses stopped altogether. The invitations stopped.

He would scroll through his phone, staring at their WhatsApp stories—laughing faces at some get-together, late-night rehearsals at the institute, a birthday celebration he hadn't even known about. The realization stung, but he told himself it didn't matter.

"They're all moving on. Good for them."

He drowned the bitterness with another drink.

Some friends left out of frustration.

"Ashu, you keep saying you'll change, but look at you, man! You're wasting yourself."

He had brushed them off with a lazy smile, waving a half-empty glass in their direction. *"Relax, yaar. I'm fine."*

Others left because they had their own battles to fight. Because they were struggling, too, chasing the same dream, facing the same failures. And they couldn't afford to carry his burden along with their own.

He didn't blame them.

But that didn't make it hurt any less.

His phone rang less and less.

When it did, it was never for the reasons he hoped.

The first time he let an unknown number go to voicemail, he ignored the nagging feeling in his gut. The second time, he stared at the screen, knowing exactly who it was—a man he owed money to.

The third time, the phone kept ringing. And ringing. Until he finally answered.

"*Ashutosh, bhai, how long are you gonna keep ignoring me?*"

"*I just need a few more days,*" he muttered, rubbing his temples.

"*Tu har baar yahi bolta hai, bhai. I was patient, but now I need my money. Do you understand?*"

Ashutosh swallowed. "*I'll get it. Just... give me some time.*"

The line went dead.

He exhaled, staring at the ceiling, his heart pounding.

There was no one left to call. No one checking in. No one asking how he was doing, what his next audition was, whether he had eaten.

His world had shrunk.

First, to the walls of his room—a place that reeked of stale alcohol and cigarette smoke, littered with discarded bottles and unopened scripts. Then, to the haze of intoxication, where reality blurred just enough to keep the pain at bay.

And finally, to the weight of loneliness. A silence so suffocating that he kept the TV on just to fill the emptiness.

And yet, even in the silence, even in the unbearable stillness of his empty world—he refused to face himself.

Looking in the mirror meant seeing the hollowed-out version of the man he once was. It meant acknowledging the dark circles under his eyes, the lost fire in his gaze, the shaking hands that had once held so much promise.

So he didn't look.

Instead, he reached for another drink.

Because as long as he was intoxicated, as long as the haze clouded his thoughts—he wouldn't have to admit the truth.

That he was losing everything.

That maybe, he already had.

ꙮꙮꙮ

The human body is resilient—but even resilience has limits.

Ashutosh had once taken pride in his strength. In the way his body carried him through grueling rehearsals, long commutes, endless auditions. He had been lean but healthy, his movements fluid, his posture confident. But now, that body felt like a ghost of what it once was.

The weight loss was drastic. His clothes, once snug, now hung loosely over his frame, the sharp angles of his collarbones protruding through his skin. His face had thinned, cheekbones more pronounced, the boyish charm he once carried now replaced by something hollow, something tired.

Dark circles framed his sunken eyes, a permanent mark of his erratic sleep cycle. Some nights, he didn't sleep at all—either too wired from substances coursing through his veins or too lost in thought to find rest. Other nights, sleep came in short, broken intervals, filled with feverish dreams and sudden awakenings, his heart pounding for no reason at all.

He woke up one afternoon—though it could have been morning or evening; time had become a blur. His head throbbed with a dull, persistent ache, and his mouth felt dry, his tongue sticking to the roof of his mouth.

Reaching for the half-empty bottle on his bedside table, his fingers fumbled, the tremor in his hands worse than before. The bottle slipped, crashing onto the floor with a loud *thud*, the remaining liquid seeping into the already stained carpet.

He cursed under his breath, pressing his palms against his temples.

The shaking had started weeks ago—at first, just an occasional tremor, barely noticeable. Now, it was constant. His hands were never steady, his grip never firm. Holding a glass of water required careful effort. Signing his name on a receipt was nearly impossible without his fingers betraying him.

One night, while standing at a bar, he had tried to light a cigarette. His hands had trembled so badly that he couldn't keep the flame steady, the lighter flickering weakly as he struggled. A guy beside him had laughed.

"Arre, bhai, just control. Is this your first time?"

Ashutosh had forced a grin, playing along, masking the humiliation. But inside, he knew. This wasn't just intoxication. This was something deeper, something worse.

The palpitations started next.

His heart would race out of nowhere, hammering against his ribcage like a warning he refused to heed. Sometimes, he would wake up gasping, his breath shallow, chest tightening as if something invisible was pressing down on him.

He brushed it off.

"Just stress," he muttered to himself. *"Just lack of sleep."*

But deep down, he knew. His body was fighting back.

His appetite had disappeared. Days would go by where he barely ate, surviving on liquid courage alone. When he did try to force food down, it sat heavy in his stomach, making him nauseous. The idea of a full meal felt foreign now.

One evening, as he stood in front of the bathroom mirror, he lifted his shirt, staring at his own reflection. His ribs were visible, stretching against his skin like a desperate protest. He ran a hand over them, pressing lightly, as if checking to make sure he was still there.

His eyes met his own in the mirror.

Who was this person staring back at him?

He knew he was spiraling.

He knew his body was suffering, breaking under the weight of his choices.

A part of him, the rational part, whispered warnings. *This isn't sustainable. This isn't who you are. This will kill you.*

But addiction spoke louder than reason.

And so, he ignored the signs.

He ignored the shaking hands, the racing heart, the sleepless nights.

Instead, he reached for another drink.

Because facing reality was still scarier than losing himself.

ᐯᐯᐯ

There always comes a moment.

A point where the spiral can no longer be ignored, where denial no longer holds weight, where reality doesn't just knock—it kicks the door down.

For Ashutosh, that moment was fast approaching.

His life had become a cycle of blurred nights and wasted days, but even in his intoxicated haze, he knew something was shifting. The consequences were no longer distant threats; they were here, looming over him, suffocating him.

And soon, they would demand to be faced.

The calls started coming more frequently. At first, he ignored them. Let the phone buzz, let the messages pile up. He told himself it wasn't urgent.

But debt doesn't wait.

One evening, as he lay half-awake on his unmade bed, the knock on his door was sharp and insistent. Not the casual, familiar knock of a friend dropping by. This was different.

He forced himself up, rubbing his temples as the pounding in his skull intensified. The knocking continued, growing louder.

"Ashutosh!" A voice rang out from the other side. Rough. Impatient.

His stomach twisted. He knew that voice.

Pulling the door open a fraction, he found himself staring into the cold, unforgiving eyes of a man he had borrowed from weeks ago. A small-time fixer who didn't believe in second chances.

Ashutosh forced a smile, his voice hoarse. *"Bhai, give me some time. I'll arrange it."*

The man's expression didn't change. *"Time? I already gave you so much. Do you even understand the meaning of today-tomorrow?"*

Behind him, another man cracked his knuckles. Silent, waiting.

Ashutosh felt a bead of sweat roll down his temple. *"Bhai, one week. Just one more week."*

The fixer's lips curled into a smirk, but there was no amusement in his eyes. *"One Week? Do you think we're running a charity?"* He leaned in, voice dropping lower. *"If you'll not return the money within a week... Mumbai is a small place."*

Ashutosh swallowed. His hands trembled at his sides, not from withdrawal this time, but from something deeper—fear.

The door shut in his face, but the message was clear.

Time was up.

His body had been screaming for a while now, but he had silenced it with alcohol, with pills, with distractions.

But there are some things even intoxication cannot mask.

One night, after another binge, he woke up gasping. A sharp pain tore through his chest, radiating to his arms. His vision blurred, black spots dancing in front of his eyes. His hands clutched at his shirt, breath shallow, heart racing so fast it felt like it might burst.

Panic clawed at his throat. *Was this it?*

He stumbled to the sink, gripping its edges as nausea surged through him. The reflection staring back was unrecognizable—hollow cheeks, bloodshot eyes, lips pale. A body on the verge of collapse.

For the first time, a terrifying thought crossed his mind.

What if I don't wake up tomorrow?

He pressed shaking fingers to his wrist, feeling for his pulse. It was erratic, uneven, a reminder that his body had limits—and he had long since crossed them.

For the first time in years, he felt something stronger than addiction.

Fear.

The worst part of hitting rock bottom isn't the pain.

It's the clarity.

Lying in bed that night, staring at the cracked ceiling of his rented room, Ashutosh finally let the truth in.

He wasn't just missing auditions.

He wasn't just losing opportunities.

He was losing *himself*.

The boy who had arrived in Mumbai with dreams so bright they could light up the night—where was he now?

The voice that had once spoken of ambition, of greatness—was now slurred, weak, barely recognizable.

He closed his eyes, the weight of it all crashing down on him at once.

If something didn't change—if *he* didn't change—

There might be no coming back.

ϷϷϷ

Ashutosh lay still, staring at the ceiling, the weight of reality pressing down on him heavier than it ever had before. The walls of his room felt like they were closing in, suffocating him in the mess he had created—empty bottles, crumpled notices, and the deafening silence of a life unraveling.

The world outside moved on without him. Roles were still being cast, films were still being made, dreams were still being chased. But he? He had become a ghost in the city he once swore to conquer.

His body ached. His mind was a storm. His soul—if he even still had one—felt lost.

And yet, in the suffocating darkness of his existence, a single, terrifying thought emerged.

Is this it?

Is this what he had fought so hard for? Had sacrificed so much for? Had left behind a life, a family, a home for?

Or was there still a chance—one last, desperate chance—to crawl out before the abyss swallowed him whole?

But the thing about addiction, about self-destruction, about reaching rock bottom, is that it never lets go easily.

And Ashutosh?

He wasn't sure if he even had the strength to fight anymore.

9

Lost Friendships, Lost Dreams

They say success is built on talent, hard work, and connections. But what happens when one of those starts slipping?

Friendships aren't just about laughter and shared experiences—they are the invisible safety nets that catch a person when they stumble. The ones who celebrate victories, but more importantly, the ones who remind you of who you are when you start to forget.

But addiction doesn't just consume a person; it consumes the relationships around them. It dulls the senses, blurs the lines between right and wrong, and makes even the most genuine concern feel like judgment. Friends try to hold on, to help, to remind—but no one can fight for someone who refuses to fight for themselves.

At first, the distance isn't noticeable. A few missed calls. A few unanswered messages. A promise to meet that never materializes. The mind creates excuses—*they must be busy, life gets in the way, things will return to normal.*

But addiction isolates. And soon, the missed calls stop altogether. The unanswered messages remain unread. The invitations stop coming.

And by the time realization sets in, by the time the loneliness becomes unbearable, it's too late. The world has moved on. The people who once mattered have drifted away.

And you are left wondering—was it them who let go? Or was it *you* who pushed them away?

At the height of his ambition, Ashutosh had believed in the power of connections—the friendships forged in shared struggles, the late-night conversations about dreams too big to fail. The people who had once surrounded him weren't just friends; they were his support system, the ones who had lifted him when the city tried to crush him.

But addiction has a way of erasing everything. And now, one by one, those friendships were slipping through his fingers.

ɢɢɢ

It started with small absences. A missed dinner here, a skipped rehearsal there. At first, no one questioned it. Everyone had their struggles, their own schedules to manage. But as the weeks passed, the pattern became impossible to ignore.

"Where's Ashu?" someone would ask at rehearsals.

"He said he had an audition."

"Again?"

A few concerned glances. A few shrugs. They let it slide—after all, wasn't this what they were all here for? To chase their dreams, to give every moment to the grind? If Ashutosh was caught up in that struggle, they understood.

But the truth was, he wasn't at auditions. Most days, he barely made it out of his room before noon. The city that had once felt like a battlefield he was willing to fight in now felt like an endless blur, a weight he was too tired to carry.

The invitations kept coming at first. Rehearsals, meetups, birthday parties. *You coming, Ashu?*

He always had an excuse.

"Sorry, man. I got a callback tomorrow. Need to prepare."

"Can't. Feeling a little under the weather."

"Next time for sure."

But there was never a next time.

The messages started piling up, unopened and ignored. At first, he told himself he'd respond later, but later never came. The longer he waited, the more awkward it felt to reply. Days turned into weeks, and soon, he had no idea how to bridge the silence.

It wasn't just about avoidance—it was the shame. Deep down, he knew they would see the change in him. He couldn't face their concern, their disappointment, the questions he didn't want to answer.

One evening, his phone buzzed again. A familiar name flashed across the screen—*Raghav Calling.*

Raghav, his closest friend, the one who had always believed in him. The one who had been there through every rejection, every late-night conversation about making it big.

Ashutosh stared at the screen. His chest tightened. He *wanted* to pick up, but what would he even say?

Instead, he let the call ring out.

A minute later, a message popped up.

Raghav: Bro, you okay? Haven't seen you in a while.

Ashutosh typed a response. Yeah, just busy.

He stared at the message for a long time before deleting it. He told himself he'd reply later.

He never did.

Days passed. The invitations slowed. The calls stopped.

His friends hadn't abandoned him. They had tried. Again and again, they had tried. But addiction doesn't just push a person into isolation—it convinces them that they're better off alone.

By the time Ashutosh realized how much he had lost, the silence around him was deafening.

ᐅᐅᐅ

In the film industry, talent alone was never enough. Reliability mattered more than dreams, discipline more than potential. Casting directors had thousands of faces to choose from—why would they wait for someone who couldn't even show up?

At first, the damage was subtle. He arrived late to rehearsals, sometimes only by ten or fifteen minutes, but it was enough to be noticed.

"Late again, Ashu?" a casting assistant had asked, half-joking, the first time it happened.

"Traffic," he muttered, running a hand through his unkempt hair.

It wasn't a big deal—until it became a habit. The ten minutes turned into thirty, then an hour. Then, some days, he didn't show up at all.

Missed calls piled up. Messages went unread.

One day, he was supposed to meet a director for a second audition—a rare callback. The kind of opportunity struggling actors dreamt of. But the night before, he had drowned himself in drinks and pills, convincing himself it would take the edge off his nerves.

By the time he woke up, the sun was already high in the sky. His head pounded, his mouth dry as sandpaper. He grabbed his phone, blinking at the time—2:47 PM.

The audition had been at eleven.

A message from his agent sat at the top of his notifications.

Agent: Where the hell are you?

He didn't respond. What could he even say? The damage was already done.

A week later, he overheard two actors talking outside a casting office.

"That Ashutosh guy? Yeah, he was promising, but he's not serious about it anymore."

"He used to be good. Now, he just looks... lost."

He wanted to tell himself it wasn't true, but deep down, he knew it was.

The industry moved fast. It didn't wait for people to get their lives together. Auditions that once came easily started drying up. The calls stopped. The opportunities that had once filled his days vanished without a trace.

His name, once murmured with promise, now wasn't spoken at all.

And just like that, he became what he had feared the most—forgotten.

ᚦᚦᚦ

Friendships don't always end in loud arguments or final goodbyes. More often, they fade—one unanswered message at a time, one missed meeting after another—until, one day, they're simply gone.

Ashutosh barely noticed it happening.

At first, it was the little things. A friend texting to ask if he was coming to a group rehearsal, and him replying, *"Can't today, bro. Next time."* But there was never a next time. A call from a former classmate, inviting him to a casual evening hangout. He let it ring, telling himself he'd call back. He never did.

They tried for a while.

"Ashu, man, where have you been? We haven't seen you in weeks."

"You okay? You've been acting different lately."

"Dude, just come out tonight, no excuses."

But addiction breeds isolation. And Ashutosh, drowning in his own mess, unknowingly pushed them away before they could leave on their own.

One evening, he found himself walking past a familiar café—the one where he and his friends used to meet after auditions, venting about directors, celebrating callbacks, laughing at their collective struggles. He hesitated, debating whether to step inside.

He finally did.

The café was just as he remembered—warm lighting, quiet chatter, the smell of freshly brewed coffee in the air. But something was different.

At a table near the window, a few of his old friends sat together, talking, laughing. For a second, he felt a surge of relief. Maybe things could go back to how they were. Maybe he could just walk over, sit down, and everything would be okay.

But then he saw it—the way they didn't even look around for him anymore. The way they laughed freely, without expecting him to be there. The way they had moved on.

He took a step forward. Then stopped.

Something in his chest tightened.

He turned and left.

The loneliness didn't come with an explosion—it crept in like a slow fog, settling over his life until, one day, he realized he had no one left.

ᚦᚦᚦ

Even as his world shrank, Ashutosh refused to acknowledge what was happening.

He had always been good at crafting narratives—after all, that was the essence of acting, wasn't it? To create believable stories, to slip into roles so seamlessly that even he could forget what was real and what wasn't. But now, the story he told himself was one of pure denial.

His friends hadn't left him—no, they had changed. They had become caught up in their own lives, their own successes, their own selfish pursuits. "They don't understand the struggle anymore. They don't get what it's like to fight for a dream."

The industry was unfair. It was all about connections, not talent. He had talent—he knew he did—but luck hadn't been on his side. It wasn't his fault. The right opportunity just hadn't come his way yet. *One big break*, that's all he needed. One director to see his potential, one role to put him on the map. Everything would fall into place then. Everything would be fine.

It had nothing to do with the fact that he had missed more auditions than he had attended. That his reputation was no longer promising but unreliable. That casting directors had stopped calling because they had long since given up on him.

No, the problem was them. Not him.

Denial was easier than acceptance.

It was easier to believe that everyone else had changed, that the world had turned against him, than to look in the mirror and see what he had become.

But the mirror had a cruel way of reflecting the truth.

One morning—if it could even be called morning—he woke up sometime in the late afternoon, his head pounding, his mouth dry. The room was dim, the curtains drawn, the air thick with the scent of alcohol and stale smoke. Empty bottles cluttered the floor, their presence a silent accusation.

He groaned, rubbing his face, trying to shake off the lingering haze in his mind.

His phone lay face down on the bedside table. When he picked it up, the screen was full of unread notifications. None of them were from the people who had once mattered.

No missed calls from old friends. No messages about auditions.

Just a few texts from unknown numbers—likely loan reminders, or people he owed money to. A couple of late-night texts he barely remembered sending. *"Hey, bro, can you lend me some cash?" "You up? Let's party." "Don't forget about me, okay?"*

No responses.

His stomach twisted, but he pushed the feeling down.

He would try again tomorrow. Things would turn around. He just needed one lucky break.

He placed the phone back down, reached for the half-empty bottle on the nightstand, and took a long sip.

Because it was easier to blame the world than to face himself.

ᕕᕕᕕ

His audition calendar, once filled with dates, times, and hastily scribbled notes, now hung on the wall like an artifact from another life. The squares were empty, the reminders long ignored. At one point, he had marked every audition with excitement, underlining important ones, circling callbacks in red ink. Now, the ink had faded, and so had his determination.

The scripts that had once excited him, that had once made his pulse race with the thrill of possibility, sat untouched in a corner of the room. Their pages curled at the edges, yellowing under the weight of time and neglect. A thin layer of dust coated them, as if they, too, had given up on him.

His once-meticulous routine—reading, rehearsing, practicing monologues in front of the mirror—had become a distant memory. There was a time when he had spent hours perfecting a single line, recording himself over and over again until the delivery felt right. Now, the only mirror he faced was the one in the bathroom, reflecting back a version of himself he barely recognized.

The fire that had once burned inside him was gone, replaced by an endless cycle of intoxication and exhaustion.

Days turned into nights turned into days again, each one indistinguishable from the last. Wake up sometime in the afternoon, if at all. Stumble through the hours in a haze, mind foggy, body aching. Find a way to numb the discomfort—another drink, another pill, another excuse. Sleep, but not really. Toss, turn, wake up gasping for air, heart pounding for no reason. Do it all over again.

The world, however, didn't wait for him.

The film industry kept moving. New actors arrived in Mumbai every day, fresh faces full of hunger and ambition, ready to take the opportunities he had once fought for. Casting directors kept holding auditions, producers kept making films, directors kept searching for the next breakout star.

His friends moved forward too. The ones who had once shared his dreams, who had struggled alongside him, were now finding their own paths. Some had landed minor roles in films or web series. Others had moved into theatre, commercials, television. They were still fighting, still pushing forward.

And the city—Mumbai, the city that had once felt like a battlefield he was willing to conquer—moved forward, indifferent to his struggles. The trains still ran, the streets still pulsed with energy, the people still chased their dreams.

But Ashutosh?

He was standing still.

Too lost to see just how far behind he had fallen.

ᕤᕤᕤ

Dreams don't die in a single, dramatic moment. They don't shatter like glass or burn away in an instant. Instead, they wither, piece by piece, slipping through your fingers so gradually that you barely notice until it's too late.

Ashutosh had once carried his dreams like a fire in his chest. He had walked through the streets of Mumbai with the certainty that he was meant for something great. That the struggles, the rejections, the sleepless nights spent perfecting his craft were all leading him somewhere.

But now, that belief felt like a distant memory.

A story he had told himself a lifetime ago.

He sat in the dim light of his rented room, surrounded by the remains of what his life had become. Empty bottles lined the floor, their presence so normal now that he barely noticed them. His bed was unmade, sheets crumpled from restless nights. The small desk in the corner—once covered in scripts, notes, and film books—was now buried under cigarette butts, unpaid bills, and unopened letters.

A script sat at the edge of the desk, untouched for weeks. He stared at it, tracing his fingers over its worn edges. Once, he would have devoured its pages, marked it with notes, practiced lines in front of the mirror until they felt like his own. Now, it was nothing more than another reminder of the person he used to be.

He had spent so long running, numbing, escaping reality that he hadn't realized what he was losing along the way.

His friends. One by one, they had drifted away. He had ignored their calls, made excuses, pushed them aside. They had tried, for a while. Asked him to meet up, check in, pull himself together. But even the most patient friends grow tired of waiting for someone who refuses to be saved.

His passion. The fire that had once driven him to wake up before dawn for auditions, to rehearse lines late into the night, to dream of standing under bright lights with the world watching—extinguished.

His future. The endless possibilities he had once seen before him, the roads that had seemed open and waiting, had slowly closed one by one. Casting calls had dried up. Directors who once saw promise in him no longer bothered reaching out. The industry didn't wait for those who lost their way.

And worst of all—

He had lost himself.

There was no dramatic realization, no sudden moment of clarity. Just a quiet, sinking feeling in his chest as he sat in the silence of his own making.

For the first time in a long time, he wondered—

When had he stopped believing?

When had he let the dream slip away?

10
Rock Bottom

Hitting rock bottom is never something you see coming. It doesn't tap you on the shoulder and whisper, This is it. It doesn't announce itself with a clear sign or an easy-to-recognize moment. Instead, it sneaks up slowly, unraveling everything piece by piece—your relationships, your ambitions, your sense of self—until one day, you wake up and realize there's nothing left to hold onto.

For some, rock bottom is quiet. A slow decay. A point of no return that they simply slip past without even noticing. For others, it's loud, messy, and cruel—a sudden, jarring moment of truth that leaves no room for denial.

For Ashutosh, it was the latter.

He had spent months numbing himself, drowning in a haze of alcohol and substances, convincing himself that things weren't as bad as they seemed. That he could fix it. That the next audition, the next opportunity, the next *drink* would somehow set things right again.

But reality has a way of catching up.

And when it did, it came crashing down in the most brutal way possible—publicly, humiliatingly, and with no way to ignore it.

It wasn't just another rejection. It wasn't just another bad night.

It was *the moment.* The one that made him see the truth. The one that made him realize he wasn't just struggling.

He was *falling.*

And unless something changed—unless *he* changed—there might be no way back.

⁂

It began like any other night—his bloodstream laced with alcohol, his mind dulled by the familiar haze. The neon lights of Mumbai flickered like distant stars, illuminating streets that never truly slept. Crowds pulsed through the city, laughter and honking blending into a chaotic symphony. But Ashutosh moved through it all like a ghost, detached, floating between the cracks of the world he once belonged to.

His pockets were nearly empty, but that didn't stop him. It never did. He leaned against a bar counter, his fingers gripping an almost-drained glass, his vision swimming.

"One more," he slurred, tapping the rim.

The bartender—an older man with a face hardened by years of serving men just like him—hesitated. *"You're already too far gone, bhai. Maybe it's time to head home."*

Ashutosh let out a bitter laugh. *Home.* What did that even mean anymore? A room in Andheri that reeked of stale alcohol and lost ambition? A place where unopened scripts collected dust, where eviction notices piled up?

He waved his hand dismissively. *"I'll pay tomorrow. Just one more."*

The bartender sighed, wiping down the counter with slow, deliberate movements. *"No more tabs. No more tomorrow."*

Frustration bubbled in Ashutosh's chest, but even anger felt sluggish now, like his body had forgotten how to hold onto any emotion other than exhaustion. He pushed away from the counter, stumbling toward the exit.

The streets outside were alive, filled with people who still had purpose, who still had somewhere to be. He envied them. Hated them.

He wandered aimlessly, his legs unsteady, his thoughts slipping in and out of coherence. The world spun, tilting sideways as he bumped into a stranger.

"Watch it, yaar!" the man snapped, shoving him aside.

Ashutosh barely registered it. He kept moving. Another bar. Another drink. Another desperate attempt to stay lost.

But his reputation had started catching up to him. The next bartender shook his head before Ashutosh could even speak. "Not tonight, Ashu. You still owe from last time."

Another door slammed in his face.

Reality was closing in.

The laughter of strangers rang in his ears, distorted, mocking. He tried to push it away, to silence the noise with another drink, another escape—but the city wasn't willing to indulge him anymore.

He staggered down a deserted alleyway, his body heavy, his mind weightless. A wall became his anchor as he slid down to the cold pavement, his breath uneven.

He had nowhere to go. No one left to call.

And for the first time, he felt it—not the numbness he had chased for so long, but something deeper.

Something terrifying.

Emptiness.

And the city, as always, moved on without him.

ﬧﬧﬧ

Somewhere in the haze of that night—whether by instinct or sheer misfortune—Ashutosh found himself outside a familiar building.

The casting office.

He didn't remember making the decision to come here. Perhaps, in some drunken corner of his mind, there was still a lingering belief that this was where he belonged. That if he could just step through those doors one more time, everything would somehow reset. Or maybe it was just another mistake in a long line of bad ones.

The building loomed over him, its bright white exterior reflecting the glow of the streetlights. He had been here before—many times. He had once walked through these doors with a script in hand, his head held high, hope thrumming through his veins.

Now, he was a different man.

His reflection in the glass door was almost unrecognizable—disheveled hair, bloodshot eyes, the shadow of stubble darkening his sunken cheeks. His shirt was wrinkled, stained with something he couldn't place, and he reeked of alcohol.

As he lurched forward, the security guard at the entrance straightened, eyeing him with suspicion. He wasn't one of the regular guards—Ashutosh didn't recognize him. Maybe that was a good thing.

The guard stepped forward. *"Sir, are you—"*

"I have an audition," Ashutosh mumbled, the words sluggish, tumbling out before he could think.

A lie. A delusion. Or maybe a wish he still refused to let go of.

The guard's brow furrowed. *"There's no audition happening at this hour."* His voice was firm but cautious. *"Do you have an appointment?"*

Ashutosh blinked, swaying slightly. The words felt distant, the meaning hard to grasp.

Appointment?

Once, he had booked them with confidence, arriving prepared, dressed in his best, his lines memorized, his hunger unmistakable.

Now?

He was a joke.

"I just..." He tried to steady himself, gripping the metal railing. *"I need to see someone."*

The guard exchanged a glance with the receptionist inside, who had started watching the scene unfold.

"Sir, you can't be here like this."

Like this.

He understood what the guard meant. *Drunk. Disheveled. Pathetic.*

But desperation had already taken hold. His pulse quickened as he took a step closer, his voice rising, slurring. *"You don't understand. I need this. Just—just one chance."*

The receptionist inside had picked up the phone, probably calling someone in charge. The guard sighed, stepping in front of Ashutosh, blocking his way.

"Please leave."

The words hit harder than he expected.

Leave.

Like he was a nuisance. A problem to be removed.

He looked past the guard, through the glass doors, at the place that had once been a gateway to his dreams. He could see people inside—assistants, casting agents, maybe even actors waiting for their turn. They hadn't noticed him. Or maybe they had and simply didn't care.

He used to be one of them. Now, he was just another struggler who had lost his way.

Ashutosh let out a bitter chuckle, though it sounded more like a choke. His chest felt hollow, his throat dry.

For the first time, standing there in the cold night air, he felt it—not just rejection, but something deeper.

Erasure.

They didn't know him anymore.

And worse—

They didn't care.

The guard's grip tightened slightly on his arm, a silent warning.

Ashutosh finally stepped back, raising his hands in surrender, his fingers unsteady. *"Fine,"* he muttered, turning away, his head spinning, his feet unsteady.

The casting office remained behind him, glowing with the light of opportunities that no longer belonged to him.

And he, a forgotten name, disappeared into the night.

ᐅᐅᐅ

Before Ashutosh could push past the entrance, the glass door swung open. A young woman stepped outside, her heels clicking against the pavement. She held a stack of papers in one hand, a phone in the other, her expression one of practiced indifference—until she saw him.

Her movements slowed. Her brows furrowed.

"Ashutosh?" she said hesitantly.

Her voice was familiar, though he couldn't place her name. He squinted, trying to force his sluggish mind to focus. He had seen her before—inside this very building. A casting assistant, maybe. Someone who had once greeted him with polite smiles when he came in for auditions.

Now, there was no smile.

Only something worse than disgust.

Pity.

A deep, unbearable pity that settled in her gaze as she took him in—the stained shirt, the unkempt hair, the unsteady stance of a man who had lost control.

Ashutosh straightened—or tried to. *"I just—I just need a chance."* His voice cracked mid-sentence, betraying him. He cleared his throat, blinking rapidly, trying to shake off the fog, the heaviness in his limbs.

She exhaled, the sound laced with exhaustion. Not anger. Not frustration. Just resignation.

"There's nothing for you here," she said.

The words hit harder than he expected.

Nothing.

Not no auditions today. Not try again next time. Not even a lie to spare his feelings.

Just 'nothing'.

His throat tightened. He opened his mouth to argue, to plead—*"I can do better, I can prove myself, just one more chance"*—but before he could say another word, the security guard stepped forward.

"Sir, I think you should leave."

A hand on his arm. A firm grip.

And then—

He was being dragged away.

Not as an actor.

Not as a contender.

But as a drunk causing a scene.

The street outside was busy, filled with people heading home from work, auto-rickshaws honking, vendors shouting about fresh fruit and hot chai.

But no one noticed him.

No one stopped.

No one cared.

A few glanced in his direction as the security guard pulled him away, but their eyes didn't linger. He wasn't worth their attention.

There had been a time when people had looked at him with curiosity, when they had wondered *"Is he someone important? Will he be famous someday?"*

Now, he was just another man lost to the city.

He wasn't a rising star.

He wasn't even a struggling artist anymore.

He was nothing.

⅌⅌⅌

A sharp gust of wind cut through the stillness, sending a shiver down Ashutosh's spine. His body tensed instinctively, but he barely had the strength to move. His limbs felt leaden, as if pinned to the pavement by the weight of his choices.

His head throbbed, a deep, pulsating pain that made it hard to think. His mouth was dry, his throat raw, his entire body aching from whatever had happened the night before. He forced his eyes open, blinking against the harsh light. The world around him was shifting from the black of night to the dull grey of morning—empty streets slowly stirring to life.

Then, the realization struck.

He wasn't in his room.

Not in his bed. Not even inside a building.

He was outside.

On the pavement.

The moment that truth settled in, a cold dread crawled up his spine. He tried to sit up, but the motion sent a wave of nausea rolling through him. He braced himself, inhaling sharply, willing his stomach to settle. His shirt was damp with sweat, his jeans streaked with dust and grime. His fingers brushed against the rough pavement, feeling the grit of the city embedded into his skin.

"How did I get here?"

His memories were hazy, slipping through his mind like water through cupped hands. He could recall fragments—a bar, drinks spilling over the edge of a glass, laughter that didn't feel like his own. The security guard's grip on his arm. The sound of people walking past him.

And then—nothing.

His breath hitched as a wave of shame crashed over him.

He had passed out. On the street.

Not in some hotel after a party. Not in the backseat of a friend's car.

He had blacked out like a man with nowhere else to go.

A few feet away, a stray dog rummaged through a pile of discarded food wrappers, its ribs visible beneath its thin fur. It tore into a leftover piece of roti, pausing only briefly to glance at Ashutosh before returning to its meal.

Somewhere down the street, a shopkeeper was unlocking his shutter. The metallic clang echoed in the quiet morning air. Ashutosh turned his head just enough to see the man step out, stretch his arms, and glance toward the pavement where he lay.

For a second, their eyes met.

The shopkeeper stared. His face unreadable. Then, he exhaled, shook his head, and went back to his business.

Ashutosh felt something twist in his chest.

No words were spoken, yet he had heard everything.

No one stopped to help.

No one asked if he was okay.

Because he wasn't. And they could all see it.

ᗡᗡᗡ

The journey home felt longer than ever. Each step was heavy, his body weak from exhaustion and dehydration. The streets of Mumbai moved around him—people rushing to work, rickshaws honking, vendors setting up their stalls—but it all felt distant, like a movie playing in the background of his own slow, painful reality.

By the time he reached his building, the sun had fully risen, casting an unforgiving light over his disheveled state. He dragged himself up the stairs, gripping the railing for support. His legs ached. His head pounded. The weight of last night clung to him like a suffocating fog.

When he finally pushed open the door to his room, the staleness of the air hit him. The place reeked of alcohol, sweat, and neglect. Empty bottles littered the floor, clothes were strewn haphazardly across the tiny space, and scripts—once his most prized possessions—sat abandoned on the desk, their pages curling from dust and time.

And then, his gaze landed on the mirror.

He froze.

For a moment, he wasn't sure who he was looking at.

The man staring back at him was unrecognizable.

His once-sharp features were gaunt, his cheekbones too pronounced, his skin pale and sallow. Dark circles sat beneath his hollow eyes, deep like bruises, stripping them of the fire they once held. His lips were cracked, his jawline rough with uneven stubble. His shirt was torn at the collar, stained with something he didn't remember spilling.

And his hands—his hands, the same ones that had once held scripts with eager determination, the same hands that had gestured with passion during auditions, that had clenched into fists of ambition—

They trembled. Violently.

He tried to still them. Willed them to stop shaking. But they wouldn't.

A lump formed in his throat. He reached out toward the mirror, fingers grazing the cold glass, as if trying to convince himself that the man before him was real.

"This isn't me."

But wasn't it?

Wasn't this exactly what he had become?

His mind drifted back, searching for the last time he had truly *tried*. The last time he had prepared for an audition, poured over a script with excitement, stood in front of this very mirror practicing his lines with conviction.

How long had it been?

A few months? A year? More?

The realization hit like a gut punch.

He had lost track.

Somewhere along the way, he had stopped counting. Stopped caring.

His reflection blurred as his vision swam with exhaustion, with something dangerously close to grief.

How had he let it all slip away?

ppp

Ashutosh stood in front of the mirror, gripping the edge of the sink as if it was the only thing keeping him upright. His reflection stared back, hollow and broken, stripped of every illusion he had once held onto. There were no excuses left to make, no justifications to hide behind.

For the first time, he couldn't lie to himself.

The world hadn't abandoned him.

He had abandoned himself.

It was never the industry's fault. It wasn't bad luck, or a lack of opportunities, or an unfair system that had conspired against him.

He had done this.

He had let the fire inside him burn out. He had chosen the bottle over the script, intoxication over preparation, escape over effort. He had pushed his friends away, ignored the calls that could have led to something, dismissed the people who had once believed in him.

And now, he was alone.

The weight of that truth settled deep in his chest, pressing down on him like a force he couldn't fight. His legs gave out, and he sank to the floor, back against the wall, knees drawn to his chest.

The room around him was a disaster—empty bottles, crumpled pages of discarded scripts, dust gathering in the corners like forgotten dreams. It looked exactly like his life: neglected, abandoned, falling apart.

His head dropped into his hands. His body ached, his temples throbbed, and his stomach churned with nausea, but nothing compared to the suffocating heaviness inside him.

The memories came rushing back. The boy from Gorakhpur who had arrived in Mumbai with stars in his eyes. The aspiring actor who had rehearsed every night until his voice was hoarse. The dreamer who had once believed he was destined for something great.

Where had that boy gone?

"Is he still in there?"

His fingers curled into fists, pressing into his temples as if trying to hold himself together. His breath came out shaky, uneven.

This—waking up on the streets, being thrown out of casting offices, watching life move on without him—
This was *rock bottom.*
And unless something changed, unless *he* changed—
There might be no coming back.

11

A Faint Ray of Hope

Rock bottom isn't a single moment of realization. It's not a dramatic, earth-shattering event that instantly leads to change. Instead, it's a state of existence—an all-consuming darkness where time blurs, hope fades, and every passing day feels like sinking deeper into quicksand. It is a place where even the smallest actions—getting out of bed, looking in the mirror, reaching out for help—feel insurmountable.

For those trapped in addiction, rock bottom isn't just about losing material things—money, opportunities, relationships. It's about losing *oneself*. It's about waking up one day and realizing that the person staring back in the mirror is a stranger. The dreams that once burned brightly have turned to ash, and the world that once seemed full of possibility has shrunk to a mere existence—an endless cycle of craving and regret.

And yet, even in the deepest despair, life has a way of demanding movement. Sometimes, it comes as a consequence too brutal to ignore—an arrest, a hospital visit, a moment of public humiliation. Other times, it arrives in the form of a helping hand, extended by someone who hasn't yet given up. But regardless of how it happens, rock bottom isn't just about hitting the lowest point. It's about what comes next.

For Ashutosh, the realization didn't come easily. He had spent too long drowning in denial, too long convincing himself that he still had time, that he could turn things around *tomorrow.* But tomorrow never came—only an endless string of wasted days, slipping through his fingers.

And then, finally, something changed.

Not overnight. Not in an instant. But slowly, painfully, through a series of moments that forced him to confront the truth. A moment of helplessness. A moment of shame. A moment of clarity.

For the first time in years, the idea of recovery wasn't just a distant thought. It was a necessity.

But wanting to change and actually changing were two different things. And as Ashutosh would soon learn, the road back would be longer, harder, and lonelier than he ever imagined.

ᐁᐁᐁ

Change didn't arrive in a single, defining moment. It wasn't some cinematic revelation, no sudden resolve that wiped away years of destruction. Instead, it came in exhaustion—the kind that settled deep into his bones, making every movement feel like dragging himself through wet cement. It came in the unbearable weight of continuing down the same path, knowing exactly where it led but being too drained to turn around.

Ashutosh's body had begun to fail him. The tremors in his hands were no longer occasional; they were constant, an unsteady shake that made even the simplest tasks—holding a glass, buttoning a shirt—feel impossible. His stomach lurched at the sight of food, rejecting anything that wasn't liquid poison. Headaches pounded against his skull like relentless waves, never truly leaving, only ebbing before returning with renewed force.

Even the alcohol wasn't working anymore.

That was the worst part.

The numbness he had once relied on, the temporary escape that had kept reality at bay, was slipping from his grasp. No matter how much he drank, how deeply he sank into intoxication, it never lasted. The brief moments of relief faded too quickly, leaving behind a hollowness that even the next drink couldn't fill. The illusion was breaking. The lie he had told himself for so long—that he was in control, that he could stop whenever he wanted—was crumbling under the weight of undeniable truth.

"If he didn't stop now, he never would."

But stopping wasn't as simple as deciding.

The first attempt at cutting back was met with merciless rebellion from his own body. The moment he tried to limit his intake, withdrawal hit him like an unrelenting storm.

It started with restlessness, a gnawing discomfort that wouldn't let him sit still. His skin burned, his muscles ached, and a cold sweat clung to him no matter how many layers he shed. Then came the trembling—violent, uncontrollable shivering that left him clutching his arms, his teeth rattling in his skull.

Nausea roared through him with no warning. He doubled over, his body rejecting what little he had consumed, retching until there was nothing left.

The nights were the worst.

Sleep was a distant memory, stolen by waves of fever and unbearable cravings. He lay in bed, staring at the ceiling, his mind screaming for relief. His limbs twitched, his chest tightened, and just when exhaustion seemed like it might take over, he'd jolt awake—drenched in sweat, heart hammering, gasping for air.

Minutes stretched into hours. Hours stretched into eternity.

This was worse than any hangover, worse than any physical pain he had ever known. His body was at war with him, punishing him for denying it what it had come to depend on.

And as the withdrawal raged on, a terrifying thought crept into his mind.

"I won't survive this."

For the first time in a long time, Ashutosh admitted the truth to himself.

He couldn't do this alone.

It wasn't just willpower or discipline that he lacked. His body was too far gone, his mind too fractured. This wasn't something he could fight in solitude, locked away in his suffocating room, drowning in his own suffering.

He needed help.

The thought terrified him.

But not as much as the alternative.

Because if he didn't reach out now, there might not be another chance.

ᛈᛈᛈ

Help didn't arrive like a savior in a grand moment of redemption. It came quietly, from an unexpected place.

The knock on his door was so faint that, at first, Ashutosh thought he had imagined it. He was curled up on his mattress, drenched in sweat, the air thick with the stench of alcohol and unwashed clothes. His head throbbed, his stomach churned, and his hands wouldn't stop shaking.

The last thing he wanted was company.

The knock came again, firmer this time.

Groaning, he forced himself to sit up, his muscles aching as if he had been in a fight. He staggered to the door, gripping the handle to steady himself before pulling it open.

And there, standing in the dim light of the corridor, was someone he hadn't seen in a long time.

A friend. A mentor. Someone who had once believed in him.

Their expression flickered between recognition and disbelief, as if they were seeing a ghost of the man they used to know. Their eyes took in the hollow cheeks, the disheveled clothes, the unkempt beard, the way Ashutosh swayed slightly even while standing still.

For a long moment, neither of them spoke.

Then, finally, the visitor let out a quiet sigh. *"Ashu."*

Ashutosh swallowed hard. His throat was dry, his voice barely above a whisper. *"What...what are you doing here?"*

"I could ask you the same thing," they replied, glancing past him into the dark, suffocating space he called home. *"This isn't you."*

Shame flooded his chest, thick and suffocating. He wanted to slam the door, to turn away, to pretend that he wasn't standing here as a wreck of the person he used to be. But the exhaustion was too deep, the weight of his own downfall too heavy to carry any longer.

He had spent so long hiding—from others, from himself, from the truth of what he had become. But now, faced with someone who still saw him, who still *cared*—he felt exposed. And the worst part?

He didn't have the strength to fight it anymore.

When the offer came—a way out, a chance at something better—his first instinct was to refuse.

He shook his head, already retreating into his familiar excuses. *"I don't need help. I just need some time. I'll get back on track."*

His visitor didn't argue, didn't push. They simply stepped inside, crossing the threshold he hadn't even realized he had left open.

Ashutosh flinched as they surveyed the room. The mess. The empty bottles. The crumpled scripts, abandoned in the corners. The shattered mirror he had stopped looking into.

"I know you, Ashu," they said finally, their voice quieter now, almost gentle. *"And I know you won't do this alone."*

His jaw clenched. The shame was unbearable.

Admitting he needed help meant admitting that he had failed. That he had lost control. That he was no longer the person he had fought so hard to be.

But his body had already made the choice for him. The tremors wouldn't stop. His vision blurred at the edges. The withdrawal was eating him alive, and he wasn't sure how much longer he could survive it.

This wasn't about pride anymore.

It was about survival.

So, finally—hesitantly, reluctantly—he nodded.

And for the first time in a long time, he let someone guide him toward the possibility of healing.

ᕬᕬᕬ

Recovery wasn't a scene from a movie where a single moment of resolve changed everything. It wasn't a straight road toward healing. It was brutal, punishing, and unrelenting.

Ashutosh had expected struggle—had braced himself for it—but nothing could have prepared him for the war that waged inside his own body.

The first night was unbearable.

The nausea came in violent waves, leaving him curled up in a fetal position on a stiff mattress. His stomach twisted and churned, but there was nothing to throw up—he hadn't eaten in over a day. The staff at the rehab center, or maybe a friend who had taken him in, had offered him food, but the thought of swallowing anything made him gag.

His body was drenched in sweat, yet he shivered uncontrollably, his limbs convulsing as if caught in some invisible battle. The blanket felt suffocating one moment and too thin the next. He tossed and turned, his skin clammy, his clothes sticking to him like a second layer of punishment.

And then there was the headache. A pounding, relentless force that seemed to split his skull in two, hammering behind his eyes, radiating down his neck. Every pulse, every throb, felt like a reminder of all the poison he had fed his body, all the nights he had drowned himself in alcohol, thinking it was an escape.

Now, there was no escape.

By the second day, the physical agony was compounded by something worse—*the itch.*

It wasn't a physical sensation, but a deep, gnawing restlessness that burrowed under his skin. His legs refused to stay still. His fingers twitched constantly. His mind screamed at him to *move*, to *do something*, to find a way out of this unbearable stillness.

He sat up, gripping the edge of the bed, his foot tapping against the floor in an erratic rhythm. His mouth was dry, his tongue thick and heavy. Every fiber of his being demanded *relief.*

Just a sip.

Just enough to quiet the storm.

His mind raced with thoughts of escape. He could walk out of here—find a bar, find a bottle, make it all stop. His hands clenched and unclenched, his breath quickened. The door was right there.

But so was the person watching him—the friend, the mentor, or maybe even a stranger who had taken it upon themselves to guide him through this. They didn't say anything, just observed, their presence a silent challenge.

He looked away, his jaw tightening.

He had never felt more like a prisoner in his own body.

The sleepless nights stretched into an eternity. He would drift off for a few minutes, only to wake up gasping, his heart racing. Nightmares clawed at him—visions of his past, of auditions he had ruined, of the people he had pushed away.

At one point, he found himself on the bathroom floor, gripping the cold tiles, his body wracked with tremors. His reflection in the mirror above the sink was a stranger—sunken eyes, hollow cheeks, desperation etched into every line of his face.

"I can't do this," he muttered, his voice barely above a whisper.

But there was no response.

No comforting words. No promises that it would get easier.

Because this was something he had to face alone.

And as much as he hated it, there was only one way out.

Through.

ᛒᛒᛒ

Detoxing the body was one thing. The process was agony, but it was *expected*—the nausea, the shakes, the restless nights. He had braced himself for the physical torment.

What he hadn't prepared for was the silence. Without alcohol numbing his thoughts, drowning out the noise, his mind was no longer his escape—it was his prison.

At first, the silence felt unnatural, suffocating. He lay on his bed, staring at the cracks in the ceiling, listening to the rhythmic ticking of the old wall clock. Time passed differently now, slower, heavier. Every second stretched into an eternity.

And then, the memories came.

His father's voice was the first to echo in his head.

"Acting? Is this a career? You always have to day dream!"

The words had been spoken years ago, but they landed with the same force, hitting him like a punch to the gut. He could still see the deep furrow in his father's brow, the disappointment in his mother's tired eyes. They had never believed in his dream—not truly. And now, he had proven them right.

He could almost hear his father scoff, *"Told you so. It'll be all a waste."*

Ashutosh turned onto his side, curling into himself. He squeezed his eyes shut, willing the voice to disappear. But it didn't.

Then came the faces of the people he had pushed away.

Rishi, who had once been his closest friend in Mumbai, the one who had celebrated his first call-back with him. They had promised to make it together—to lift each other up. But when Rishi had tried to help him, tried to tell him he was losing himself, Ashutosh had lashed out.

"You're teaching me?" he had spat, reeking of whiskey. "What have you achieved in the industry more than me?"

That was the last time Rishi had tried.

And then there was Meera.

Meera, who had once believed in him more than he had believed in himself. Who had spent hours helping him rehearse, who had told him he was meant for something big. Who had watched him crumble and had begged him to fight back.

"I'm your friend, Ashu. Can't see you like this," she had said, her voice breaking.

But he had been too deep, too lost. Instead of holding onto the people who had tried to save him, he had pushed them away.

Now, as he lay in this unfamiliar room, sober for the first time in years, there was no one left.

But the worst wasn't the voices of his past.

It was *his own voice*.

"I just need a chance."

He had whispered those words outside a casting office, drunk and desperate, before being dragged away like a nobody.

He had once walked into such offices with confidence, his heart pounding with excitement, his hands gripping a script that he had rehearsed a hundred times.

Now, he couldn't remember the last time he had prepared for anything.

The reality was unbearable. He had betrayed the one thing that had ever given his life meaning.

For years, alcohol had been his shield, his escape. Whenever regret crept in, whenever the weight of failure pressed against his chest, he had drowned it in another drink.

Now, there was nowhere to hide.

No bottle. No intoxicated haze. No temporary numbness.

Only himself.

The regret was suffocating, clawing at him from the inside out. He wanted to run. Wanted to scream. Wanted to disappear.

But for the first time in years—

He had to *sit with it.*

᭞᭞᭞

There were moments when Ashutosh was sure he wouldn't make it.

The first few days had been brutal—his body had turned against him, punishing him for depriving it of the poison it had come to depend on. The sweats, the shaking, the nausea—he had expected all of that. But what no one had prepared him for was *the voice*.

The voice in his head that whispered, *This is pointless.*

"You're already finished, Ashu. Just go back. One drink, and everything will be okay."

The craving wasn't just a physical ache—it was a shadow that followed him, lurking behind every thought, waiting for the smallest moment of weakness. He could almost feel the cold glass in his hands, hear the familiar clink of ice, the burn down his throat.

It would be so easy.

He could just *walk out*.

The streets of Mumbai were still out there, waiting for him. The neon-lit bars, the hidden alleys where he had spent so many nights, the faces of people who wouldn't judge him because they were drowning too.

"Just one more time."

The thought was terrifying—how quickly his mind could rationalize his own destruction.

He thought about leaving more times than he could count.

There were nights when he sat by the door, staring at the handle, convincing himself that no one would stop him if he just stood up and walked out. He had enough money for one drink. That was all he needed. Just one.

"What's the point of all this?" he muttered to himself, voice hoarse from exhaustion.

But then, the memory of that pavement returned—the cold, hard ground beneath him, the way people had stepped over him like he was nothing.

The casting office. The pity in the assistant's eyes. The security guard's firm grip, dragging him away like a drunk causing a scene.

The realization that he had become a ghost, someone the world had already moved on from.

"I can't go back to that," he whispered, almost as if saying it out loud would make it true.

And so, somehow, he stayed.

Not because he was strong.

Not because he believed in himself yet.

But because the alternative—going back—terrified him more than the pain of staying.

There were no grand moments of inspiration, no sudden bursts of motivation that made recovery easier. But somewhere, deep beneath the exhaustion, beneath the cravings, beneath the self-hatred—

There was something.

A flicker of something he thought he had lost.

The tiniest voice, buried beneath all the others.

"I just need one more chance."

Not from the industry. Not from his friends.

From himself.

And that was enough—just barely, but enough—to keep him from walking away.

ৡৡৡ

Recovery wasn't a single battle—it was a war fought in inches, in painfully small victories that no one else would notice.

There was no grand moment of transformation. No dramatic epiphany where everything clicked into place and the past stopped haunting him. The struggle remained, lingering in the quiet moments, in the long hours of self-doubt, in the weight of everything he had lost.

But there were small moments, barely perceptible shifts in the way the world felt.

One morning, he woke up and realized he had slept through the night—no violent shivers, no sweating through his sheets, no waking up gasping for air, heart pounding in panic. Just sleep. It had been years since his body had truly rested, and the unfamiliar stillness felt almost unnatural.

Then, there was the first meal that didn't make him sick. For weeks, his stomach had rejected everything, punishing him for depriving it of alcohol. But one afternoon, he took a bite of simple dal and rice—and kept it down. It didn't taste like much, but it felt like something.

And then, the biggest moment of all—a morning where he woke up and didn't immediately crave a drink. It wasn't a dramatic realization, just an absence of something. The need that had ruled his every waking thought for so long had loosened its grip, if only for a few hours.

These victories were small, almost invisible. But to Ashutosh, they meant everything.

He wasn't healed. Far from it. His body still felt weak, his mind still fragile. The weight of his past hadn't lifted; it still clung to him, a constant reminder of the damage he had done—not just to himself, but to those who had once believed in him.

He had no idea what lay ahead.

The film industry had moved on without him. The friends he had lost weren't waiting for his return. The dream that had once burned so brightly inside him now felt like a distant memory.

But for the first time in years, he wasn't stuck in place.

He had taken a step forward.

And for now, that was enough.

12
The Last Drink

The night was quiet, unusually so—an eerie stillness that felt unnatural for a city like Mumbai. Normally, the streets outside his window never slept. The restless hum of traffic, the occasional burst of laughter from passersby, the distant thumping of some late-night club—all of it merged into the familiar rhythm of a city that never truly stopped. But tonight, the world outside felt distant, as if muffled by something unseen.

Inside, the air in his room was thick, heavy with the scent of stale alcohol and something more intangible—regret, perhaps. The dim yellow bulb above cast long shadows on the walls, distorting everything, making the already small space feel even more suffocating. It was as though the room itself was holding its breath, waiting.

In the center of the table, motionless and unassuming, sat a single glass.

Half-filled. Untouched.

The amber liquid inside shimmered under the weak glow, catching the light in a way that almost made it look inviting. Almost.

Ashutosh sat in front of it, unmoving. His fingers hovered just above the rim, hesitant. He could feel the coolness of the glass even without touching it, could already taste the familiar burn that waited beyond the first sip.

But he didn't lift it. Not yet.

It was strange how something so small could carry so much weight. It wasn't just a drink. It was a decision. A reckoning. A final moment that stretched infinitely in both directions—past and future converging at this single point in time.

The past was loud in his head. It crashed over him in relentless waves—the years of struggle, the endless cycle of auditions and rejections, the slow unraveling of his dreams. He had once believed in himself, in his talent, in the promise that hard work and perseverance would lead him somewhere. But somewhere along the way, hope had turned to exhaustion, and exhaustion had turned to escape.

And now, here he was.

A man at the edge of himself.

There was nothing between him and his thoughts now. No distractions, no numbing agents, no excuses. Just this—this moment, this choice, this drink that waited for him.

And for the first time in a long time, he realized—

What happened next was entirely up to him.

ᗩᗩᗩ

Memories came in waves, relentless and unfiltered, crashing over Ashutosh with a force that left him breathless.

The first was a warm one—Mumbai, the city of dreams, revealing itself to him in a blur of flashing billboards, honking taxis, and an overwhelming sea of people. He had stepped off the train with nothing but a backpack slung over his shoulder and a crumpled piece of paper in his hand, filled with scribbled addresses of casting agencies. The air had smelled of rain and street food, a strange mix of hope and chaos.

"Bhaiya, Andheri chaloge?" he had asked a cab driver, his voice barely masking his excitement.

The man had looked at him, then at his worn-out shoes, and chuckled. *"Naya aaya lagta hai?"*

Ashutosh had only smiled. He had been too hopeful, too alive to care about the knowing look the driver gave him—the look reserved for all the fresh-faced dreamers stepping into the city's unforgiving embrace.

But hope, he learned, had a way of withering.

The next memory hit harder—the suffocating heat of a crowded audition room, the murmured conversations of desperate actors waiting for their turn, the weight of unseen judgment pressing down on him.

"Next!"

He had walked in, heart pounding, palms slick with sweat. The casting director barely looked up from his phone as Ashutosh began his monologue. He had poured his soul into those lines, had given them everything. But when he finished, all he got was a disinterested nod.

"Thank you. We'll be in touch."

They never were.

The polite rejections had been easy to endure at first. They had felt like stepping stones, part of the journey. But then came the not-so-polite dismissals—the curt dismissals, the cold glances that said everything without a word.

"Sorry, we're looking for someone with a more established profile."

"You're good, but not quite what we're looking for."

"Maybe try TV serials?"

He had smiled through the rejection, swallowed his disappointment, told himself that the next one would be different. But as months turned into years, the rejections weren't just professional—they were personal. Each one chipped away at him, wore him down, left him feeling smaller.

He remembered the nights spent rehearsing in front of his cracked mirror, whispering lines to himself, convincing his reflection that one day, someone would see him. Really see him.

But the city hadn't seen him.

It had swallowed him whole.

Then came the drink.

At first, it had been nothing more than a way to take the edge off. A single sip after another rejection. A small indulgence to quiet the gnawing fear that he wasn't enough. But then, that single sip had turned into two, then three, then a bottle, then numbness.

And now, here he was.

He exhaled slowly, his gaze fixed on the glass before him. The amber liquid barely rippled, as still as the room around him, as if waiting for his decision.

Was this who he was now?

Just another name added to the long list of dreamers who had come to Mumbai and lost themselves?

His fingers twitched, reaching—hesitant, uncertain. The weight of everything he had once been, everything he had lost, sat heavy in the air.

He had always thought that if his life had a defining moment, it would be in front of a camera, under the bright lights of a film set. Not this. Not in a dimly lit room, staring at a drink that could decide his fate.

The past had already been written.
But the future?
The future was waiting.

ᚦᚦᚦ

Ashutosh ran a hand through his unkempt hair, his fingers lingering on his temples as a dull ache pulsed through his skull. The silence in the room was deafening, the kind that pressed against his chest and made it hard to breathe. It hadn't always been this way.

There was a time when his phone buzzed constantly—calls from friends, messages from fellow strugglers about auditions, invites to late-night chai sessions after long, exhausting days.

"Bro, got a lead on a new project. Want to tag along?"

"You coming to rehearsal tonight?"

"Let's meet at Prithvi, talk scripts over coffee."

He used to be part of something. A circle of dreamers, all chasing the same impossible goal. They had laughed together, suffered together, celebrated the smallest victories like they were winning Oscars.

And then... things changed.

The messages became fewer, but not because they had stopped caring. It was him.

He had stopped responding.

"Ashu, you okay? Haven't heard from you in a while."

"Come on, man. Let's meet. We miss you."

"Pick up your damn phone."

He had seen them all. Read them. Ignored them.

At first, he told himself he was just busy. That he needed space. But the truth was uglier—he was drowning, and instead of reaching for help, he let himself sink.

Then came the harder conversations. The ones where they tried—really tried—to pull him back before it was too late.

"You're not yourself, Ashu," Rohan had said one night, sitting across from him in a dimly lit bar. *"You don't come to auditions, you barely leave your room. This... this drinking every day—it's not normal, man."*

Ashutosh had scoffed, taking another sip of his whiskey. *"I'm fine."*

"No, you're not," Rohan had insisted, his voice laced with frustration. *"We all struggle, but this? This isn't struggling. This is giving up."*

Ashutosh had laughed bitterly. *"You think you're better than me, huh? Just because you landed a couple of roles?"*

Rohan's face had fallen, hurt flashing in his eyes. *"That's not what this is about."*

But Ashutosh had already waved him off. *"You don't get it. No one does."*

After that, the calls became less frequent. The invites stopped coming. One by one, they had let him go—not because they wanted to, but because he gave them no choice.

Even his mentors, the ones who had once seen something in him, had stopped checking in.

"Ashutosh, you have talent, but talent means nothing if you won't fight for it."

"I can't keep recommending you when you don't even show up sober."

"You're wasting it, kid."

And now, here he was.

No one left to text him. No one left to knock on his door, force him out of his own misery. No one left to stop him from doing what he was about to do.

The realization was crushing.

He had done this to himself.

He reached for his phone, fingers hovering over the screen. Maybe... maybe he could fix things. Maybe it wasn't too late. He scrolled through his contacts, stopping at familiar names—Rohan, Aditi, his old acting coach. He thought about calling. About saying something, anything.

But what would he even say?

"Hey, sorry I ruined everything. Can we pretend like the last two years never happened?"

He clenched his jaw and locked the phone, setting it aside.

This was his reality now. His consequence.

No one was coming to stop him.

No one was left to pull the glass from his hands.

This was his decision.

And his alone.

ᛈᛈᛈ

Ashutosh stared at the amber liquid, the dim light from the overhead bulb making it glisten inside the glass. It looked harmless. Almost beautiful.

"A single drink won't ruin everything."

The thought came unbidden, a familiar whisper in the back of his mind.

He could almost hear his own voice from a hundred nights before.

"Just one more. Just to take the edge off."

"It's not a big deal. I can stop whenever I want."

"I deserve this. After everything, don't I deserve something?"

Each time, he had believed it. Each time, he had taken the first sip thinking it would be the last.

But it had never been just one.

He clenched his jaw, his fingers twitching as they hovered near the glass. The weight of his own weakness pressed against him.

He had told himself before that he was in control. That he chose to drink.

But wasn't that the biggest lie of all?

Control had slipped away from him long ago.

His mind flashed back to the moments he had tried to forget—the humiliating nights stumbling through the streets, the slurred apologies to people who had stopped believing them, the mornings spent shaking and sick, desperate for the next fix just to feel normal again.

His breathing grew uneven. He pulled his hand back slightly, curling his fingers into a fist.

"What difference does it make?" a darker voice in his head argued. *"You've already lost everything. One drink won't change that."*

But hadn't that always been the problem?

It did change things. Every time he gave in, it set off a chain reaction—one he couldn't stop once it started.

His heartbeat pounded in his ears.

He could already imagine it. The moment the alcohol burned down his throat, warm and familiar. The brief rush of relief. The illusion of peace.

"And then?"

Then the second drink.

Then the third.

Then the morning after, waking up in a place he didn't recognize, his body aching, his mind blank except for the shame curling in his stomach like poison.

His breathing grew ragged.

He had come so close to crawling out of this hole.

Did he really want to fall back in?

His fingers reached forward again, brushing against the cool surface of the glass.

And then—

He hesitated.

For the first time in a long time, he hesitated.

ᗧᗧᗧ

The question loomed over him like a storm cloud, thick and inescapable. His fingers brushed against the cool surface of the glass, tracing the condensation forming along its edges. The liquid inside barely rippled, as if waiting—*expecting.*

"*What happens after this drink?*"

The answer should have been simple.

One sip, and the cycle would begin again.

The haze would return, swallowing his thoughts, numbing the pain. One night would bleed into another, and before he knew it, weeks—maybe months—would disappear into an alcohol-soaked void. He would wake up in places he didn't recognize, with people who didn't care, drowning in the same self-inflicted misery he had barely crawled out of.

The progress he had made, however fragile, would shatter. The pain of withdrawal, the struggle of facing his demons—wasted.

The people who had once believed in him? They had already given him second chances. Some had given him third, fourth, and fifth chances too. Would anyone still be there to pull him back if he fell again?

Or would this drink be the one that finally severed his last ties to the life he had once dreamed of?

But *not* drinking—that was terrifying in its own way.

Because if he put the glass down, if he walked away, he had no guarantee that things would get better.

The emptiness inside him might not vanish overnight. The struggle to rebuild his life could be harder than simply giving in. Sobriety wouldn't hand him back the years he had lost, nor would it suddenly make him the actor he had once aspired to be.

What if he was too late?

What if he had already missed his chance?

What if the damage was already done, and no matter what he chose now, he was still doomed to be just another forgotten name in a city that chewed up dreamers and spat them out?

His pulse pounded in his ears.

There was no easy answer.

There was only *this moment*.

And the choice before him.

ﭖﭖﭖ

He lifted the glass.

The movement felt natural—*too* natural. His fingers curled around the smooth surface, the chilled condensation dampening his skin. The liquid inside shimmered under the dim light, rich and golden, reflecting his hollowed-out eyes in distorted swirls. It was waiting for him, calling to him in the way it always had.

A single sip. That was all it would take.

The familiar warmth promised to settle into his veins, to quiet the relentless thoughts that clawed at his mind. It would numb the weight of his past, blur the edges of his regrets, hush the fears of his uncertain future. It had always been there for him, never judging, never questioning—just *there*, offering an escape.

His breathing was shallow, uneven. The glass felt heavier than it should, as if the choice it carried had physical weight.

The world outside moved on without him—cars honking in the distance, a faint murmur of voices seeping through the thin walls, the city alive and uncaring.

And here he was, trapped in a single moment.

The weight of the decision pressed down on him, heavier than anything he had ever carried.

Was this the end?

Or was it a beginning?

His fingers tightened around the glass.

ᗡᗡᗡ

Outside, the city carried on, unaware.

The neon lights flickered, casting restless shadows against the pavement. Distant voices wove into the hum of late-night traffic, a symphony of lives moving forward. Somewhere, a car engine sputtered to life. Somewhere, laughter echoed down an alley. Somewhere, a dream was beginning, or maybe ending.

Inside, the glass hovered just inches from his lips.

The golden liquid trembled, catching the dim glow of the room. His fingers tightened around the glass, knuckles pale, breath shallow. The silence stretched, thick and unyielding.

Time didn't move—only his thoughts did, unraveling in chaotic whispers.

The weight of years sat heavy on his shoulders. The relentless auditions, the echo of rejection, the faces of people he had pushed away. The nights spent chasing a feeling that never lasted. The mornings filled with regret. The exhaustion of it all.

And yet, in the stillness of this moment, something else stirred. A flicker of something he couldn't quite name.

The answer lay somewhere in the pause.

A second passed.
Then another.
Outside, a streetlight buzzed.
Inside, his hand remained steady.
The city murmured. The glass waited.
And then—
Darkness
and
The Last Drink

When I first set out to write **The Last Drink**, I didn't know exactly where the story would take me. I only knew that I wanted to explore something raw, something real—the quiet battles people fight behind closed doors, the weight of unfulfilled dreams, and the thin line between hope and self-destruction.

Ashutosh's journey is not just about addiction; it is about the relentless pursuit of something greater, the crushing blows of failure, and the slow, painful realization of how easy it is to lose oneself. His story is a reflection of so many untold stories—of struggling artists, of dreamers who arrive in big cities with nothing but ambition, and of those who turn to vices to silence the voices of doubt.

Addiction is rarely a loud, dramatic fall—it's a slow descent. It creeps in, disguising itself as relief, until one day, it becomes impossible to live without. That's what I wanted to capture: not just the external struggle, but the internal war—the excuses, the self-deception, the guilt, and the overwhelming desire to escape. Because for many, addiction isn't just about substance abuse. It's about avoiding pain, numbing regret, and filling the void left by dreams that feel too far away.

I wanted this book to feel honest, to capture the desperation, the moments of fleeting joy, and the terrifying uncertainty of trying to change. Recovery is never linear. It's messy, painful, and often filled with moments of relapse or doubt. But at its core, it is about choice.

That's why The Last Drink doesn't give a clear resolution. Because in reality, there are no simple endings—only the choices we make in our darkest moments. Some find their way back. Some don't. And some remain suspended in that fragile in-between, where one decision can tip the scales either way.

This book is for anyone who has ever felt lost. For those who have struggled with addiction, with failure, with the feeling of being invisible in a world that never slows down. And most of all, for those who still hold on to the faintest sliver of hope, even when everything seems to be slipping away.

Thank you for stepping into this story with me. I hope it stays with you, lingers in the spaces between certainty and doubt, and makes you think about the choices we make—and the ones we don't.

— Kunwar Ankur

Author's Biography

Kunwar Ankur was born in Gopalganj, Bihar, and raised in Lucknow, Uttar Pradesh, shaping his perspective with a rich blend of both cultures. From an early age, he found solace in words—writing poetry, weaving stories, and capturing the unspoken emotions of life. His passion for storytelling deepened through his studies in mass communication, allowing him to explore narratives that are raw, real, and deeply human.

His literary journey began with **Charag** (March 2021), a Hindi poetry collection that delved into themes of love, longing, and introspection. The book struck a chord with readers who saw reflections of their own emotions in its verses.

With **The Last Drink**, Kunwar Ankur ventures into fiction, painting a hauntingly real portrait of addiction, ambition, and the fragile thread that separates downfall from redemption. This novel isn't just a story—it's an experience, a journey through the highs and lows of chasing dreams in a city that often swallows them whole.

But this is just the beginning. He continues to write, to explore new ideas, and to craft narratives that leave a lasting impact.

If his words resonate with you, connect with him:

Instagram: kunwar_ankur_

Email: info@kunwarankur.com

Website: www.kunwarankur.com

Your thoughts, feedback, and conversations mean everything. Join the journey, and let's keep the stories alive.